THE KILLING

Corruption is running rampant between members of government and powerful businessmen: bribery, conspiracy, and illegal dealings. Henry Quinlan, sent by Senator Howard Beauchamp to investigate, patiently compiled a dossier of evidence against the culprits. When he dispatched his documentation to the senator by train, protected by two Pinkerton detectives, it was stolen en route — and Quinlan disappeared. Now Jason Brand has been called in to track down both the dossier and its author. But someone's determined to stop him . . .

NEIL HUNTER

THE KILLING DAYS

Complete and Unabridged

LINFORD
Leicester

First published in Great Britain in 2016

First Linford Edition
published 2017

A catalogue record for this book is available
from the British Library.

ISBN 978–1–4448–3485–7

Published by
F. A. Thorpe (Publishing)
Anstey, Leicestershire

Set by Words & Graphics Ltd.
Anstey, Leicestershire
Printed and bound in Great Britain by
T. J. International Ltd., Padstow, Cornwall

This book is printed on acid-free paper

Prologue

It began when Frank McCord sent for Brand and came directly to the point, which was his way. He saw no profit in wasted effort, so the minute Brand joined him in his office introductions were made and McCord went straight to the reason he had sent for Brand.

'This is Senator Howard Beauchamp. One of the few men who understands and supports our existence. He's here because the President has made it clear he wants our help on an important matter.'

Beauchamp held out a hand and Brand took it. The Senator had a strong grip. It went with his solid appearance. A stern but good-looking man in his early fifties. An imposing, well dressed man. Beauchamp held Brand's inquiring stare. The Senator had a slight smile on his lips as *he* stared back.

'Now we have each other's measure, Mister Brand, I have the feeling we will get along.'

Brand relaxed as he sat back, facing the Senator in front of McCord's desk. There was something about Beauchamp he found interesting.

'The Senator has a problem requiring our expertise,' McCord said.

Never heard it called expertise, Brand thought. He did not voice his thought.

'This has been going on for some weeks,' Beauchamp said. 'It began when what I can only describe as rumors began to reach my ears. Isolated items that when added up piqued my interest — and my suspicions. Enough for me to set one of my investigators on to the matter. Good man I've come to trust. Name of Henry Quinlan. Works best on his own. Keeps things close so not to arouse any unwanted attention. Quinlan spent a few weeks on the matter, reporting only to me.'

The Senator held out a picture of the man called Quinlan. It was an official photograph taken from the file Beauchamp had with him. Quinlan looked to be a good looking man in his mid-thirties. A thin mustache adorned his lip and his thick head of dark hair gave the appearance of being unruly.

Beauchamp paused to take a drink from the half-filled tumbler of water in front of him. He glanced at McCord and gestured for him to step in.

'Quinlan's initial investigation showed the presence of extreme corruption involving both businessmen and members of government. Individual conspiracy together with illegal dealings. Hidden fraud that is resulting in government contracts with the gained money being shared between those involved. People in high positions manipulating large amounts of money. Favors being offered and bribes taking place. Quinlan obtained names from people who knew about these dealings but were unable to do anything because, simply, they realized they couldn't trust those in higher authority in case they were part of the conspiracy.'

'Sounds as if these people have tight control of the situation,' Brand said.

'Exactly,' Beauchamp said. 'It's difficult to point the finger when you can't be sure the one you're confiding in isn't part of the deal.'

McCord said, 'Henry Quinlan's investigation began to explore a number of possibilities. He employed his expertise to convince those with individual knowledge to write down what they knew. He gathered his evidence and had it legally notarized. He gathered this evidence from a number of sources and once he had what he considered enough for the Senator to use, he arranged for it to be sent to Washington.'

'I received a telegram from him saying he was sending the evidence by train, protected by a two-man team of Pinkerton detectives,' Beauchamp said. 'He did this because he told me he felt he was being watched. His idea was to draw anyone following him away.'

The pause in Beauchamp's speech warned Brand of a problem.

'Anything else you can tell us, Senator?'

'All I can tell you now is that Quinlan appears to have vanished. The Pinkerton men sent a message they felt they were vulnerable riding the train and they were going to leave it and pick up a couple of horses on the next stop. Place called Handy, Texas. The Pinkertons have been ordered to stay in Handy until you arrive and assist. It's a precaution as we can't be sure who to trust.'

'Getting to Handy isn't as easy as crossing the street,' Brand said.

Beauchamp said, 'Fastest way would be by rail.' He caught the skeptical look in Brand's eyes. 'Not by a regular service. Frank, may I make use of your telegraph?'

McCord led the Senator out of the office. Brand was left alone to wonder just what the hell they were up to. The pair were gone for over forty minutes until McCord came back on his own.

'You fancy a fast train ride?' He

didn't wait for Brand to answer. 'Gather what you need from your quarters. Beauchamp is offering you a ride to the rail depot. Take in what he tells you and then make the most of the next hours. I'll let the law in Handy know you're coming. He'll be expecting you. May I suggest, Brand, that you maintain a strict silence on details of the matter. The Senator hasn't said it in so many words, but I suspect there may be those who could be working against him.'

Brand didn't ask any questions. He knew McCord well enough not to raise any kind of objections. He made his way to his room, packed his gear and weapons. Ten minutes later he was seated beside the Senator in the man's private carriage and wondering just what he was letting himself in for.

By the time they arrived at the Washington rail depot Brand had been given chapter and verse on the Senator's accomplishments since he and McCord had deserted Brand.

Beauchamp's influence, coupled with

the free use of his relationship with the President, had got things moving with unexpected speed. A powerful steam locomotive, a ten-wheel gleaming black machine, sat on a spur line. It had a single coach attached to the tender. It sat waiting for its single passenger, smoke coiling from the stack and steam hissing from its valves. Beauchamp had a conversation with the engineer and his fireman, nodding and shaking hands with them before he rejoined Brand.

'If it can be done this is the crew and the locomotive. We are basing the length of the journey on average speed and stops only for taking on water and fuel. The engineer, Jenks, understands the urgency and he has estimated the distance to be in the region of 1300 miles. He says he's aiming for fifty hours at the outside, less if he can keep up the pace.'

'I like his optimism,' Brand said.

'Telegrams have been sent to clear tracks of any trains that might get in your way. It's going to take a deal of organizing, but once it was stressed the requests came from the President himself there were only minimal objections.'

Brand raised a hand to the engineer as the man hauled himself up into the locomotive. He would be in hands of the two men operating the train once it moved off. He walked to the steps of the coach, sensing Beauchamp close behind.

He handed Brand an envelope. 'Expense money. You may need it. Be embarrassing if you didn't have any.'

'You need receipts?'

Beauchamp gave a hearty laugh. 'No, I don't think that will be necessary. Now I have every confidence in you,' the Senator said. 'So it seems does Frank.'

'Nice to be well thought of,' Brand said.

'It's important that information is brought to Washington. We have to weed out this corruption before it seriously damages public confidence in the government. Henry Quinlan has made great efforts to gather these witness statements. It must not be wasted.'

'If McCord is sure I can help we can all sleep easier tonight,' Brand said.

Beauchamp managed a slight smile. 'Do I detect a sense of cynicism there, Mister Brand?'

Brand stepped up onto the coach. He dropped his gear on the platform and glanced down at the Senator.

'Ask McCord how I feel,' he said. 'He seems to know me pretty well.'

THE HUNT

1

There were four riders sitting motionless on the approach to the rail depot at Handy, Texas. The day was blisteringly hot. Heat waves shimmered in the air. When the object of their interest appeared, rolling along the tracks and heading for the depot, the riders moved. They closed in on the isolated depot, taking their time, so that as the locomotive and its three cars slowed, the riders came from behind the wooden building and reined in. Pale fingers of dust followed in their wake, hanging in the still air. Steam billowed from the locomotive as it stopped. The cars shuddered, couplings clanging as they came to rest. The fireman climbed over the tender and reached up for the nozzle of the water chute. He swung the chute into position and started to fill the locomotive's tank. The engineer leaned out the cab window, dragging off his stained cap. He was sweating. There was little escape from the heat. At the rear of the train the conductor stepped down from the baggage car and wandered over to the depot office to talk to the manager. He barely had time to open his mouth before one of the four riders appeared at his side. The man was wielding a large revolver and he held it so both men could see it.

'Son, there ain't any kind of money on this train,' the conductor said. 'If that's what you came for I opine you will be disappointed.'

The man waggled the barrel of his revolver in the direction of the telegraph key. 'You — yank out them wires,' he said.

The manager did as he was told. He watched as the man leaned in through the window, took hold of the wires and pulled hard until the other end tore free from the junction box on the wall.

'Wouldn't want you affixin' them

back in a hurry,' he said. 'You got any guns in there?'

'In the drawer. Just the one.'

'Hand her over.'

The man took the short-barreled pistol and tucked it behind his gunbelt.

'I don't have one,' the conductor admitted.

The man opened the conductor's uniform coat and checked for himself. 'Just to make sure,' he said.

He leaned back and gave a loud whistle. It brought his three companions into view. They reined in next to the idling train. Two dismounted and climbed into the passenger car. The fourth man remained in the saddle, holding the reins, a long-barreled Henry rifle trained loosely on the loco's driver and fireman.

The depot manager was looking nervous and the man with the gun noticed this.

'*What?*'

'Someone might show up from town.'

'You expecting anyone?'

'Not especially but sometimes the marshal walks out to check things.'

The town stood less than a few hundred yards from the depot. A straggle of buildings. Corrals and cattle pens. The gunman glanced in the direction of the town. He could see figures moving about but there was nothing to suggest anything out of the ordinary.

'If he's got any sense he'll be sitting somewhere cool,' he said.

The pair who had climbed on board the train appeared, stepping down to the ground and returning to their horses. One of them held up a leather case. It looked like a doctor's medical case, only larger.

'Let's go,' he said.

'You got it?' the gunman asked, stepping away from the conductor.

'We got it.'

The incident might have ended there if the depot manager had stayed his hand. But he was a proud man, dedicated to his job and though he

16

hadn't shown it outwardly, he was angry at what these four men were doing. In all his years as manager of the rail depot nothing like this had ever happened and he was not going to let anyone say Clem Dobson had failed in his duty.

He had not be entirely truthful about the armament he had in his office. Handing over the revolver he had allowed his gaze to flicker to the stubby Greener resting on wooden pegs over the top of the window frame. Double cut-down barrels, loaded with 12-gauge shells, the shotgun was within easy reach.

As the gunman let his gaze flicker in the direction of his mounted partners Dobson reached for the Greener, snatching it free and angling the black muzzles in the direction of the man. It was a reckless move, doomed to failure, because Dobson had to ear back the hammers before he could fire, and the gunman was a shade faster. His pleasant smile faded as he moved the muzzle of the already cocked Colt, eased back on the trigger and put a big .45 caliber lead slug into Dobson's chest.

The solid slam of the slug kicked Dobson away from the window. He uttered a single cry of pain as the slug burned into this body, snapping rib bones and tearing into his heart. His right thumb slipped off the single hammer he had pulled back and his finger curled around the trigger in a reflex action. The Greener boomed, a gout of flame and smoke issuing from the barrel as it discharged its load. The full force of the shot hit the conductor in the face, blasting it away in an instant. The conductor's head blew apart like an overripe melon.

Before the conductor's near decapitated body hit the platform, the rider holding the rifle opened fire. He shot the loco's engineer when he leaned out of the cab, then turned his weapon on the fireman as the man scrambled for cover. Two .44–40 rifle slugs hit him between the shoulders. He stumbled and fell, dropping from the water tank and hit the ground hard.

'*Goddam it,*' the man with the leather case yelled. 'Let's move, let's move, before that hick town lawdog wakes up.'

The man on the ground ran to his horse and hauled himself into the saddle. The four riders reined about, cut across the tracks and sent their horses off to the west, out across the wide expanse of the Texas Panhandle country.

*   *   *

By the time the town Marshal, Earl Hicks, arrived at the depot he found a scene of utter chaos. Four dead outside the train. When he took himself, pale faced and sweating, nothing at all to do with the heat, inside the train he found two more dead men. Both these men were found in the private Pullman coach that sat between the passenger coach and the baggage car. They had both been savagely knifed and had their throats cut. The surviving passengers from the single coach were expectantly shocked.

Marshal Hicks ran a quiet town. Little happened in Handy. The only time it came close to being rowdy was when the hands from the outlying ranches came in at the end of each month to spend their pay. The rest of the time Handy was just another Texas town going about its everyday business, serving those very same ranches. Earl Hicks had taken on the post of Marshal five years earlier, after serving the original lawman as deputy for ten years. Hicks knew his job and would have been the first to admit it was easy pickings. The previous Marshal had steered Handy through the tough years and on retirement he had handed over to Earl Hicks.

'Take care of my town now, Earl. I done tamed her down so all you got to do is make sure she don't get stirred up *again. Don't you mess up, son, else I'll have to come back and kick your ass.'*

Hicks was never certain whether his old boss had been joking, or meant what he said. In the event Handy caused him no kind of problem. It was a small town a long ways from anywhere and nothing of any consequence happened there.

Until today.

It was an unqualified mess. The one thing Hicks hated more than anything was a mess. He stood with his hat in his hand, wiping the back of his sweating neck with his already sodden neckerchief, staring at the dead and wondering just what the hell he was supposed to do.

'*Earl?* Hey, Earl, what should we do?'

It was his deputy, a lanky youngster called Toby Books. His normally healthy pallor had turned a grayish white and he was trying not to retch.

Hicks cleared his throat, realizing this was his problem. It was what he was paid to deal with.

'Yeah, all right, Toby. I want you to

get back to town. Fix it with Bernstein to get down here with his wagon and move the bodies to his parlor. While you're up there have Doc Gillard come take a look at them first.'

Glad to have an excuse to leave Books caught up his waiting horse and headed back to town, leaving Hicks to deal with the agitated passengers. The Marshal was reprieved briefly when Harvey Stoner showed up. Stoner was the relief depot manager. After looking at the dead, Stoner vanished inside the depot to check out the telegraph. He opined it would take him a couple of hours to get the wires reconnected.

'You get that done soon as, Harvey. I need to get the word out what's happened here.'

With that task under way Hicks went to speak to the passengers. He had decided all he could do was have them taken into town and housed in Handy's hotel until arrangements could be made to send them on their way.

It was about to become a long day.

2

Forty-six hours later Jason Brand stepped down from the special train that had brought him to Handy. It was early morning. He felt lightheaded as he stepped from the coach and walked down to the locomotive to shake hands with the crew who stared at him through red-rimmed eyes, faces grimed and sweating.

'That was some wild ride, fellers,' he said. 'Much appreciated. Now you go sleep it off in the hotel. Courtesy of Senator Beauchamp. Everything on the house.' He stepped back to look over the gleaming, dirt-streaked locomotive. 'Hell of a beast you got there, Mister Jenks.'

'She is that, son, and proud of her.'

Brand made his way into Handy, still taking in the hectic ride he'd spent in the coach. Beauchamp had made sure it had been supplied with food and drink for the trip so Brand hadn't gone hungry. The Pullman coach had been equipped with a compact kitchen and he had been able to make himself coffee on the installed stove. It made him appreciate how the wealthy lived.

From Washington the special had rolled through the empty miles of Virginia, picking up the pace as they moved west and south, diverting to spur lines and main tracks. Tennessee and on into Mississippi and through Louisiana and finally crossing into east Texas. Along way the train paused only to pick up water and fuel, resting for short periods so the crew could take coffee and food from Brand. Then on again, building up speed as they pushed ever forward. Through changing landscapes. Some green. Others showing miles of emptiness. Flashing by isolated settlements and across the miles that brought them ever closer to their final destination. Smoke and sparks steamed from the loco's stack.

For Brand, with nothing to do but endure the hours, he found himself thinking about the two people who meant so much to him.

Virginia and Adam. With little else to fill his mind he concentrated on them. Wishing he was with them and wondering how long it might be until he was with them again.

He had no idea how long that would be. The week he had spent with his son Adam had been reasonably relaxed, following the events in New Mexico. Shortly after meeting Adam for the first time with the revelation the boy was his son, Brand's mission had taken him into the high mountains. A hoped-for routine mission had become a desperate struggle to stay alive, a teaming with the bounty man Bodie, and his son showing up in the middle of the deadly confrontation with the Monk clan, had made Brand aware his life was at odds with bringing up Adam.

When it had been over, allowing Brand time with his son, a possible solution offered itself when Brand and Adam journeyed to New York and a meeting with Virginia Maitland. The business heiress, who had shared a dangerous mountain trek with Brand, was working at restoring her inherited empire and also cementing her relationship with Brand. They had both realized their feelings for each other and wanted to maintain it. Virginia had business matters to attend to that were going to demand she returned to England for some months. To Brand's relief Virginia had been only to willing to have Adam accompany her when he had told her about his son and his concern for his well-being. Although Adam had been worried over her reaction he had taken to the young woman immediately. During the time they spent in New York, with Virginia showing them the city and introducing them to people she knew, Adam responded well and the proposed sea voyage across the Atlantic had sparked his imagination. By the time Brand returned to Washington,

Virginia and Adam were on their way. He admitted to himself it was a great relief to know his son was safe and in good company.

He found he was reliving those events. With little to distract him it became inevitable he would do just that.

Time passed. Brand did his best to relax but found it hard. He was not a man who took to idleness. He needed to be involved. Being trapped in the carriage's confines was something he found discomforting. He drank a few glasses of the expensive whisky Beauchamp had supplied. Not enough to get drunk, but of sufficient quantity to make him relax and eventually sleep. He slept long and hard, waking to darkness and a heavy rainstorm. He stood at the closest window and peered out. Pouring rain hit the glass. Lightening forked over the low crown of hills they were speeding through. He felt the carriage rock under his feet. Idly wondered where they were but didn't pursue the thought.

The hours went by. Brand settled, then paced. Slept some more. Stretched his legs and spoke to the crew when they halted at some stop in the middle of nowhere to take on more water. The events took place a number of times as they gathered the long miles under the wheels of the train.

And then they were in Texas. Their destination still a distance away but seemingly in sight. Finally the last stretch along a lonely line that ran through a dusty landscape that leveled out to an empty plain beneath a wide, brassy blue sky, where the heat took on a relentless intensity.

Handy came into view. A straggling clutch of weathered buildings. Signs they were in cattle country in the holdings pens. Corrals and freight sheds. The locomotive slowed and came to a steam billowing stop . . . and Brand's arrival in town went unnoticed . . .

The rail depot had an empty feeling to it. A window boarded up. No one around. After his leave-taking of the train Brand walked up into Handy and picked out the hotel. He stepped up onto the boardwalk and went into the lobby.

The man behind the desk glanced up. He had a weariness in his manner Brand couldn't figure.

'Name of Brand. You should have a reservation for me. It was wired in.'

The man simply nodded, turned and took a key from the hook and passed it over. Brand signed the register. The key was handed over and Brand made his way up the stairs and located the room. He dropped his bag on the floor and crossed to the window, sliding it open to allow some fresh air in. Glancing across the street he spotted the Marshal's office. That would be his first call. Brand decided to freshen up first. The last stretch of his journey had been long and dusty. He took off the coat of his black suit and draped it across the bed, loosened his tie and opened the top button. There was water in the jug on the wash stand. He tipped some into the bowl and sluiced his face. As he raised his head he caught sight of himself in the mirror. His image stared back at him. Brand ran a hand across his face, feeling the stubble there. He needed a shave. In fact he needed a hot bath. His visit to the lawman could wait a while. He slid into his coat and went downstairs, asking the clerk about the availability of a hot bath.

'Freeman's barber shop and bathhouse is just along the street. Take a left out the door.'

Still the same distracted tone.

Brand followed the directions and went into the establishment. When he stepped out an hour later he was clean shaved and considerably cleaner. Soaking out the stiffness from his train ride Brand felt a whole lot better. While he'd been soaking the barber had his assistant brush down Brand's suit and shirt. He was feeling almost human again. He decided he was ready to face the town's lawman and crossed the street.

Brand had noted the same atmosphere in the barber's shop. Not the usual chatter from the man. He didn't make anything of it — not right then. Not until he met and spoke to the town's lawman.

The office was no different to a hundred others Brand had been in. Functional. The furniture battered and ready for changing. The walls plastered with town regulation notices and wanted flyers. Pot-bellied stove supporting a blackened coffee pot issuing flavored steam. A gun rack on the wall next to the scarred and occupied desk.

Handy's Marshal glanced up from a document he was reading as Brand stepped inside.

'Marshal Hicks? Jason Brand.'

Hicks pushed to his feet, reaching out to take Brand's outstretched hand. He was a quiet-looking man, with graying hair and showing a slight paunch.

'Weren't certain sure when you was arriving,' he said. 'Even so I'm glad you're here. Truth be told I ain't ever had to handle anything like this afore. Handy is a peaceable place. You know what I mean?' Hicks gestured for Brand to sit down.

'Seems I'm missing something, Marshal. You want to tell me. Supposed to be meeting a couple of men here. You know where they are?'

Hicks froze for a moment, then said, 'You won't have heard. Traveling and all.'

'I guessed there was something the way people have been acting.'

'Train that arrived yesterday was hit by armed men. Train crew was shot down, so were the station people. Two fellers in the special coach dead as well. Telegraph wires were pulled so we couldn't send anything out until they were fixed. Soon as they were working again we got messages coming in. One of 'em said we should expect you. Seems your people had been expecting those two dead men to stop off here.'

'They were Pinkerton agents.'

'I know that now,' Hicks said.

Brand nodded, settling into a chair that actually had a padded leather cushion and back.

Hicks maintained a constant flow of chatter as he attended to the coffee. It was out of pure nervousness. The man was way out of his depth and had the grace not to conceal it. He handed Brand a thick china mug as he walked back to his desk and sat down.

'I was deputy to the town marshal and took over when he retired three years ago. There were some rough times back then but Jim Tanner handled it. By the time he handed over the job this town was so quiet it was hard to believe. Haven't had a shooting in years. Then to have this happen. Well, I can tell you, sir, it set the town on its ear. Not just a shooting. It was pure slaughter. Never seen the like before, an' I hope to never again.'

Brand tasted his coffee. It was the first drink he'd had since alighting from the train.

'Good coffee, Marshal.'

'Hell, son, it's Earl. And thank you for the compliment. Now what can I do to help you?'

'Tell me what happened.'

'Six people dead is what happened. Mister Brand, I'm just a cowtown lawman. I'll admit I ain't used to this kind of mess. And, hell, I never had so many telegraph messages since I don't know when. First I get told you're on your way and to let the detectives know when the train shows up. Only before we know it we have the train held up and people killed. Damnit, Mister Brand, I know'd the engineer and the fireman. Both good men. Same as the conductor and the station master.' Hicks gulped his coffee down, shaking his head. 'And it's not like I'm going to forget the way those Pinkerton fellers died. Throats cut like they was hogs in a slaughterhouse.'

Brand could see how visibly shaken Hicks was by what had happened in his quiet, dusty town. Rowdy cowboys on a Saturday night was most likely the height of excitement in Handy.

'This took us all by surprise,' Brand said. 'Intention was a peaceful meeting with those Pinkertons before we headed out.'

'If this was supposed to be such an all fired secret,' Hicks said, 'how come those men knew those Pinkertons were coming to Handy to meet you? How come? Tell me that, Mister Brand?'

Brand had no immediate answer to Hicks' question. He knew one thing for certain. Senator Beauchamp had an informant in his department. Someone able to learn about the meeting and pass it along to his contacts.

He realized he needed to get in touch with McCord and let him know. Beauchamp was going to have to do some careful checking of his own people. It suggested that the group he was up against were organized enough to have someone in the Senator's camp.

'I'll take a walk to the telegraph office,' he told Hicks. 'I need to let my chief know what's happened.'

'I'm sure you need to do that.' Hicks paused before asking the question both of them knew was coming. 'Mister Brand, I understand from the way Washington acted there must have been something real important on that train. You know about it and can you tell me?'

'There was and I'm not able to divulge what right now. Nothing personal, Earl, just the way I've been instructed.'

'Fair enough,' Hicks said, obviously disappointed. 'Can't add much more myself, but I can send for Toby Books and you can have a talk to him. Books is my deputy. Young feller, but a damn good tracker. He lit out after the *hombres* who done the crime and followed them until their trail vanished. That be a help, Mister Brand?'

Brand nodded. 'Could be helpful.'

'Time you get back from sending your message I should have Toby here.'

The office was still deserted when Brand returned from sending his report. He helped himself to more coffee and sat down again, and stretched his legs out.

The office door opened and Earl Hicks came in, followed by a tall, lean younger man in dark pants and a Nankeen shirt that hung loosely on his slim torso. He had his hat in his hand and thick, dark hair tumbled across his forehead. As Hicks had said, Toby Books was young, his amiable face unlined and smooth. That didn't faze Brand. He judged people by their actions, not their age.

'Mister Brand, this is Toby Books.'

Brand stood and took the deputy's outstretched hand. The man's grip was firm and genuine.

'Glad you're here, sir,' Books said. 'Hope I can be of help.'

'How far out did you follow those tracks, Mister Books?'

'Near full day. Until they just naturally played out. Lost 'em when they hit hardrock.'

Brand indicated a map pinned to the

wall behind Hicks' desk. 'You show me where?'

Books crossed and stood at the map. He took a minute to establish the location, then placed a finger on the paper.

'They took off more or less south. Kept in that direction for as long as I could track them.' Books was nervously toying with the brim of his hat. 'Hate to admit I lost 'em after that.'

'Don't feel bad about it, boy. You did well enough.'

'One of their horses had a bad shoe. Right foreleg. Looked like it might have had a split in the metal. Left a distinct mark.' He glanced at Hicks, then back to Brand. 'That any help, Mister Brand?'

'Could be a real big help, Toby. Now, if they were to keep on south are there any places they might stop off? Towns? Way station?'

Hicks crossed to the wall map and traced a line with his finger.

'There's a town here,' he said. 'It's smaller than Handy. Called Little

Creek on account of the actual crick that runs by on its way to the Brazos. It's more of a supply place than a town. Big store that supplies cow outfits in the area.'

'Hey, don't forget Blanco,' Books said.

'Ain't likely to forget that hog wallow,' Hicks said. He tapped his finger on the map below Little Creek. 'Way I see it a bunch of no-goods who hit that train would feel right at home at Blanco. No law. The sort of place where a man can mix with his own kind and forget civilized rules, if you get my meaning.'

He returned to sit at his desk.

'Have to say you've given me some good pointers,' Brand said. 'I'm obliged to you both.'

'Mister Brand,' Hicks said, 'if you do stop off at Blanco you watch yourself. I called it a hog wallow. That was a disservice to hogs, if you know what I mean.'

'I'll watch my back, Marshal, and

thanks for the advice.'

Brand studied the map, looking beyond the spot Books had indicated.

'Nothing much out that way,' Hicks said. 'Lots of empty country before you reach Mexico. You think they might be headed over the border?'

'They stole something off that train and the suspicion is they knew what it was they were taking,' Books added.

Hicks saw Books was about to say something more. 'No point asking, Toby. I already did but Mister Brand here is not at liberty to tell us what was taken.'

Books looked disappointed.

'Sorry, Books, I got my orders.'

Books shrugged. 'Well, nice to have met you, Mister Brand. I better get back out there. Work to be done. Good luck to you.'

The deputy left the office.

'Sound young feller,' Brand said.

'That he is,' Hicks said. 'You plan on picking up that trail and seein' where it takes you?'

'Yeah. Right now that's all I got.'

'Any more I can do,' Hicks said, 'you just let me know.'

'Point me in the direction of the best livery in town. I need to rent a good horse.'

'I'll do better. Jake Converse has the best horses in town. We can walk down to his place now.'

Leaving the office they made their way to the west side of town and the big, well-maintained stable. Hicks led the way inside and introduced Brand to the owner. Jake Converse was in his early fifties, a rawboned individual with a bald head and a large, drooping walrus mustache. His sturdy work clothes hung on his skinny frame.

'Good to know you, Mister Brand,' he said. His voice was soft, his words clear though. When he took Brand's hand his grip was surprisingly powerful.

'Jake, Mister Brand needs a good horse. Now against my better judgment I told him you were the best horse dealer in town, so don't you let me down.'

That brought a genuine laugh from Converse. 'Hell, Mister Brand, if I even imagined he meant even one word, I'd be mortal offended.'

'I'm in your hands, Mister Converse.'

'Hell, son, it's Jake. People start calling me *Mister*, I start to worry I'm getting' old.'

'I'll leave you two to make your deal,' Hicks said.

'You a lawman?' Converse asked as he led Brand into the depths of the livery. 'Just curious is all.'

'Kind of,' Brand said.

Converse a hand across his bald head. 'Not bounty man else Earl wouldn't have been so polite.' He paused in mid-step. 'You to do with the US Marshal office?'

'Somewhere south of that. I work out of Washington. Justice Department about covers it.'

Converse's eyes took on a conspiratorial gleam. 'Well hell son, don't need to say more. Come to look into that killin' at the rail depot? Poor Earl ain't got a

42

notion how to handle it. Not that he could be blamed. It were all done and dusted by the time he got to the station. Young Toby followed the tracks until they wore out. Mebbe you wonder why Earl didn't gather a posse and go after those fellers?'

'Be truthful I'm glad he didn't. From the way that robbery went that bunch was pretty hard.'

'This is a small town. People are good at the work they do, but there ain't one of 'em fit to go chasing a gang of killers. Earl didn't have the where-withal to suggest it. Anybody else got hurt he'd never live with himself. Anyhow, that's my opinion for what she's worth.'

'Seems I should have come straight to you,' Brand said.

Converse grinned. 'Son, ever'body talks to me. They come for their horses and naturally we talk things over. Just like we're doin'.'

He led Brand to a stall where a big, powerful-looking brown and white paint horse stood. The animal swiveled its head and walked to the gate.

'Good sign,' Converse said. 'Now she don't take to everyone, but damned if she doesn't have that gleam in her eye. I think she'll take to you.'

Brand reached out to stroked the paint's muzzle. The horse didn't back off. It pushed back against his hand.

'She's one hell of a horse, mister. Got enough bottom to ride all the way through Mexico and back. Now she can be feisty, but use firm hand and she'll do what you want.'

'What do you call her?'

'Why *Lady*, what else,' Converse said, ''cause that's what she is.'

The paint lifted its head at the sound of its name, shaking it soundly and made a soft sound.

'She'll do right well,' Brand said. 'Fit me up with a good saddle and all the trappings. A *good* saddle. I have a notion we're going on a long ride.'

They completed their deal and Brand paid the price. He left the livery and made his way to a general store he'd seen earlier. He needed to buy himself provisions and additional gear for his ride. His remark about a *long ride* had not been off the cuff. Something told him he was going to go a long way in his attempt to regain what had been stolen from the train the day it had been subject to the robbery.

When he returned to his hotel with his purchases the first thing he did was change from his suit into more suitable clothing. Dark pants and a gray shirt. A soft leather vest went over the shirt. He had a spare shirt in his saddlebags and he added a couple of boxes of ammunition he'd bought for the .45 Colt and the .44–40 Winchester. A sheathed knife was threaded onto his belt. The adapted Colt .45, with its short barrel and shaved down butt went into one pouch of the bags. He had bought a couple of large canteens that would supply his water needs. In his possibles bag he had cooking gear and food. Brand had treated himself to a handful of slim cigars and some extra Lucifers wrapped in a strip of oilcloth. In addition was a blanket roll and a long, black slicker in case the weather turned. Brand packed everything neat and tidy.

On his way out he handed in the key.

'You leaving town already?' the clerk said.

'Yeah, work to do.'

Some damn work, he thought.

Brand shouldered his gear and stepped outside. He turned in the direction of the livery, eyes searching the street as he walked. There was little to interest him. Just a scattering of Handy's citizens going about their business.

Handy.

A nice, ordinary town that had suffered a brutal act of violence a few days ago. The shadow would stay with the town for some time. But it would survive Brand knew. Hopefully any further consequence of the attack would take place elsewhere. Far away from Handy. The town didn't need any more problems. It was down to Brand to make sure it stayed that way.

He met Hicks as he neared the livery.

'You all set?'

'As I ever will be.'

Hicks followed him inside to where Converse had Lady saddled and waiting. He secured his saddlebags and fixed his blanket roll and possibles bag in place.

'Good luck,' Converse said after shaking Brand's hand.

'I wish there was more I could offer,' Hicks said.

'My job now,' Brand said as he swung into the saddle and gathered the reins.

Hicks raised as hand as Brand gigged the paint into movement and rode out of the livery.

Along the street Toby Books was sitting on a sturdy chestnut, waiting.

'Mind if I ride a while with you? Show you the way they went?'

'Obliged,' Brand said and they moved off.

They crossed the rail tracks and headed away from town.

Brand sensed his companion had something on his mind. He figured Books would spit it out when he was ready so he didn't ask. They had covered a couple of miles before Books spoke.

'It true you were a US Marshal?'

'Checking up on me, boy?'

'Just curious, is all. You mind me asking?'

'It goes back a ways now.'

'Jake Converse told me. Said he recalled your name and that you'd worn the badge.'

Brand grinned. 'That old man knows too much,' he said.

'It true then?'

'It's true.'

'Why did you leave?'

'Didn't Jake know that? It's all old history now. I guess I overstepped the line and the ones in charge took against me. Made it so I couldn't stay on.'

'I didn't mean to pry . . .'

'Like I said it's over and done. I

48

survived. Moved on. In the end I was offered this second chance and took it. Lot's happened since then.'

'Good things I hope.'

'Some,' Brand said. 'Can't say all of it bad.' He thought of Adam and Virginia. 'And some even better.'

Books reined in, indicated the way ahead with a sweep of his arm.

'You stay south,' he said. 'Aim for that ridge ahead. Keep it in your line of sight. Can't prove it out but I'm pretty certain that's the way they were heading.'

'Thanks for your help, Toby. Appreciate it.'

They shook hands.

'Good luck, Mister Brand.'

'It's Jason to my friends.'

Books swung his horse around and headed back towards Handy.

Brand sat and surveyed the way ahead. He leaned forward and stroked the paint's neck.

'You and me now, Lady,' he said. 'Let's go see what we can find.'

3

Lander was becoming more and more restless. His partner Dane Mennard could tell because he was smoking cigarettes continuously. It was the giveaway sign. Now Mennard had no such problems. He was content to sit back and enjoy the peace and quiet. It wasn't that he was lacking in ambition, just satisfied to let it arrive in its own time. Sitting it out and waiting in the stand of trees and brush where they could observe the fading trail left by the rest of the bunch was an easy way to pass time, but Lander was starting to exhibit a dissatisfaction with the task.

Mennard topped up his mug from the coffee pot set over the small fire.

'Before you ask,' Lander snapped, 'no I don't need any more coffee. I drink much more I'll turn into a damn bean.'

'Why, Vince, we gettin' a little touchy?'

'What do you think? Costigan sends us all the way back here to keep a watch. *For what?* Nearly two days and we ain't seen a damn soul. It's like we're the only living things around. There's no regular trail hereabouts so why would we see anyone?'

'Lige is just being cautious. He doesn't want some posse catching up with us.'

'If there was going to be a posse they would have showed by now. Come on, Dane, that town ain't got the means to chase after us. They got too much caution after what we done.'

'Doesn't mean they haven't sent out the word. US Marshal office. Mebbe Rangers.'

'Well Handy is a distance from any-where. Take time to bring anyone in if they are coming. And that works for us. Longer it takes the better chance we have of disappearing.'

Lander finished rolling a fresh ciga-rette. He scratched a match on his gun butt and lit up, blew out a coil of smoke.

'Sure, that's fine for Lige and the

others. They're making distance. We're back up the trail. Kind of leaves us out on a limb.'

Mennard grinned. 'You feeling left out?'

'What I'm feeling is I got a target on my back.' He arched his stiff body. 'Just how much longer we going to sit out here?'

Mennard swirled the coffee in his mug. 'Come morning we'll ride. Catch up with the others.'

'About damn time,' Lander grumbled.

He turned about, changing his mind about coffee and took a step before freezing on the spot, his left hand raising his rifle.

Mennard saw his move, snatched at the pistol holstered on his hip.

'*You see him?*' Lander said.

'Yeah, I see him.'

They watched the single rider coming towards them. He was sitting relaxed in his saddle, astride a strong-looking paint. The rider, though, appeared to be checking his way. His head moved constantly, eyes cast down.

'He's looking for tracks,' Lander said, 'and I don't mean cattle tracks.'

'Certainly interested in something,' Mennard agreed.

'I say he's looking for our prints. Damnit, Dane, can't be anything else. Like I said we're way off the regular trails. Costigan came this way because hardly anyone cuts this piece of country. That feller ain't looking for daisies.'

Mennard couldn't fault his partner's reasoning. The approaching rider was checking the ground intently now. The way he was acting was proving out.

Leaning forward Lander brought his rifle to his shoulder, sighting along the barrel, his finger resting lightly against the Henry's trigger.

'You just keep coming, friend,' he murmured. 'Way you're acting is making me suspicious . . . no doubt at all . . . '

Mennard gripped his Colt. Watched the rider getting closer.

'No way he's getting close,' Lander said in a whisper. 'I'll put him out of that saddle first . . . '

4

The ride out from Handy had given Brand the opportunity to learn about the paint. He quickly found the horse was sharp and responsive. Lady settled into his presence with little resistance. She moved well, head held high, and it was plain she was more than ready to take him wherever he wanted. Brand made sure to keep praising her, leaning forward to stroke her silky neck and offer words of encouragement. The closeness between horse and rider was important Brand understood and the paint showed her pleasure by giving him an easy ride.

The afternoon was slipping away. The weather still warm, with hardly any breeze. Brand knew that once the light began to fade he was going to lose the tracks he was following. Toby Books had put him on the right trail and

Brand had been able to follow it even though the ground prints were becoming more indistinct all the time. His ability to maintain his search would prove harder once he reached the hard ground Books had mentioned. Difficult, but not impossible. It would just take him longer to pick up the trail again. He had noticed one shoe print that showed a split in the metal. Just as Toby Books had mentioned. *Smart boy*, Brand thought. A keen eye and a good brain.

The undulating landscape, dotted here and there by islands of timber and brush, caused Brand to ride with ears and eyes alert. He was not by nature a nervous man, simply cautious. That caution had kept him alive so far and he had no thoughts to lessen his awareness of his surroundings, taking in sights and sounds and assessing anything that might stand out from the norm.

He hadn't seen a solitary soul since leaving Handy. That in itself was not unexpected. This was lonely country, greatly uninhabited, so lonesome travel was an accepted part of it. Which did not deter Brand from remaining sharp.

He was in sight of a stand of timber now, the shadowed interior of the trees and brush offering no easy view of anything that might be concealed within.

As good as Brand's awareness was it fell far short of that of the horse he was riding. It was Lady who reacted to something, her head turning slightly in the direction of the stand. Brand felt the horse hesitate, breaking stride as she slightly pulled back. He heard the agitated blow of air from her nostrils as Lady picked up a scent, a warning tremor coursing through the powerful body.

If he hadn't received that equine warning he might not have taken close notice himself, but as he did Brand picked up the briefest flicker of the lowering sunlight glance off the barrel of a long gun as it pushed through the greenery.

Brand reached and grasped his

sheathed Winchester, hauling it from the scabbard as he slid his feet from the stirrups and rolled out of his saddle. He landed on his feet, reaching out to slap the paint on her rump.

'*Get out of here, Lady.*'

The horse veered to the side, Brand cutting away, and as he moved he heard the solid crash of a rifle shot. Heard the thump as the lead slug burned into the ground feet away. He had been looking in the direction of the concealed shooter and caught a glimpse flame as the rifle fired. He dug in his heels and kept moving, weaving from side to side, firing from the hip, levering and firing a couple more times at the spot where he had seen the gun flash.

Then he dropped, using a slight depression in the ground to provide a degree of cover. Brand propped himself on his elbows and sent a tight group of shots into the trees. He had no idea how many men were concealed by the timber, just put the shots out to discourage any reckless moves.

* ★ ★ ★

'*Sonofabitch*,' Lander said. 'He hit me.'

He clutched a hand to his right shoulder where one of the random shots had burned a searing line across the flesh.

'*Stay the hell down then*,' came Mennard's less than sympathetic reply.

Dane Mennard had never been one to temper his feelings, even when he was talking to his partner. The burst of gunfire had been unwelcome and if Lander hadn't been so quick to take a shot at the rider, they might have been left alone. All that had changed the minute Lander had taken his shot albeit off target. Now they were in the position of having to take on the rider, who was far from being a novice.

'What the hell you taking it out of me for?' Lander said.

'If you'd kept your finger off the trigger he might have ridden by.'

'And mebbe not.'

Lander pulled further back into the brush.

'What you doing now?'

'I'll cut through to the far side. Come at him from there.'

Mennard didn't bother to argue. He knew Lander's stubborn nature. Once he got an idea in his head there was no stopping him. Mennard hoped the move worked because if it didn't the rider might push matters his way and . . .

How the hell did we get in this bind? Mennard thought.

Mennard was no stranger to situations such as this. He had been forced to get himself out of awkward holes on other occasions. Yet he knew that with each successive encounter the odds were shortening and one day he would not walk off free and clear.

Lander's quick trigger finger had drawn them into this. All because he couldn't wait. Because he was an impulsive chancer. It wasn't the first time Lander had messed up. Well maybe this time he would end up with a lead slug in his butt.

There was a flurry of movement in

the trees and brush off to Mennard's right. That would be where Lander had gone. The flurry increased. Then a rifle shot. A fast response followed by a harsh yell that trailed off into a fading groan.

Mennard knew the sound came from Lander. The unseen rider had taken him. He clutched his Colt, the palm of his hand slick with sweat. Mennard didn't consider himself a coward but he held respect for his own life. The last thing he wanted was to lose it out here in the backyard of nowhere. He was worth more than being gut shot and left for dead in this godforsaken piece of emptiness.

★　★　★

Brand had moved, knowing the hidden gunmen might converge on his position. He was sure he had winged one of them but he needed to be sure. He pushed into a crouch, then ran forward and moved around the clump of timber and brush, expecting the sound of shots to follow. None did and he pushed into the surrounding cover of the greenery, figuring that his sudden move had caught the opposition off guard.

So far in and he dropped to a crouch, stilling all movement as he focused on his surroundings. He pulled the Winchester close not wanting to allow it to disturb the brush. Even a slight sound could carry and betray his position. He waited. Listening for anything that might give away the positions of whoever had shot at him. It was possible they were doing the same. Which might result in a stalemate.

Then he picked up a disturbance off to his left and ahead. The low sound as someone moved briefly. Followed by a groan that was cut off quickly. He pinpointed the direction. Moved quickly in that direction. Brand transferred his rifle to his left hand and slid the Colt from his holster. The crowding bulk of the brush could easily get in the way of a long gun, and truth be told Brand was faster with the Colt. He paused briefly to establish his bearings, head moving left to right. Eyes searching . . . and that was when he saw the hunched shape on the ground no more than ten feet away. Then out the corner of his eye he picked up movement coming in from his right. The bulk of a man. The shape of a hand gun emerging from the shadows. The muzzle angling in his direction. Brand turned from the hip, the Colt following through and he fired. Cocked the gun and fired a second time. The other man's gun fired off a single shot as he went down on his knees, throwing his left hand across to steady his gunhand. Brand fired off two more shots, the heavy slugs thumping into the man's chest, tumbling him to the leaf-strewn ground. He arched once, body straining before he stretched out. The back of his shirt began to bleed red from the twin exit holes.

Smoke curled up from the muzzle of Brand's handgun as he watched, waited, and realized there was no more to come. There had only been the two of them. He moved to check out the man he had just put down. A brief inspection told him the man was dead. Brand moved to the first man. He heard the harsh rasp of breath as he stood over him. The man's chest was wet with blood and there was more over his right hip. Sensing Brand's presence the man lifted his head, sweat gleaming on his face. He looked at the still form lying a few yards away.

'*Vince?*'

'He's dead.'

Brand stepped in close and took away the man's rifle and handgun.

'Not about to leave me a chance.'

'Game's over. You lose, friend.'

Brand leaned over and took hold of Mennard's shirt. He dragged the man over to the base of a tree and propped him in a sitting position. Mennard made a hurt sound, staring up at Brand with undisguised hostility.

'Now what do we do?'

'I could look at your wounds. Looks like a bad chest hit. Not much I can do.'

'Hell, that don't sound promising.'

'I'm not in the promising business.'

Mennard pressed his hand to his bleeding side. He could feel warm blood seeping between his fingers. He knew he was hit bad and he was too far away from anything resembling help.

'It looks bad,' he said. 'Now I suppose you'll tell me I got what was coming to me.'

'Sounds like you already know that.'

'*Jesus*,' Mennard said, 'I'd hate to get on your bad side.'

Brand moved through the brush to where the coffee pot was still steaming on the fire. He filled a tin cup and brought it back to hand to Mennard.

'I been drinking this stuff the last couple of days,' Mennard said. 'Decided I'd had enough, but right now it's welcome.'

Brand pulled a thin cigar from his pocket, lit it and handed it to Mennard. The man drew heavily, letting smoke dribble from his lips.

'Having a hard time figuring you,

mister. First you shoot me and now you're handing me all the comforts of home.'

Brand brought himself a cup of coffee and hunkered down.

'This where I tell you all my secrets?' Mennard asked.

'Tell me if I miss anything,' Brand said. 'You waited for the train to stop at Handy. Shot down a bunch of people and took what you came for. I'm guessing you and your partner were waiting here to pick off anyone chasing after you and giving the rest of your bunch time to move on.'

Mennard said, 'And I'm figuring you know what was in that case we took.'

'Reasonable assumption.'

'If Vince hadn't been so loose with that trigger there might have been a different outcome.'

'We'll never know.'

Mennard drained his coffee, held the cup out to Brand. He refilled it.

'I need to know,' he said. 'You the law, or a bounty man?'

'Not doing this for a reward.'

'Can't decide whether that's better than taking a slug from a bounty man.'

'In the end it's a piece of lead is all.'

Mennard started to groan from the pain. He managed to empty his coffee cup then let it drop from his fingers. He leaned his head back against the tree and stared up at the blue sky through the canopy of branches.

'*Look at that . . .* ' he said, his voice strangely gentle. '*Nary a cloud in sight . . . a grand day . . .* '

His eyes stayed wide open as his last breath came. The cigar in his hand drifted smoke.

★   ★   ★

Brand cleared the trees and went to find Lady. The paint was no more than a few yards away. Contentedly cropping at a patch of grass. She raised her head at Brand's approach, waiting while he gathered the reins and led her back to

66

the trees. He tied the reins to a low branch, stroking the animal and praising her.

Then he went back to where the bodies lay, moving on to where their horses stood. He stripped off saddles and removed the bridles and all the other trappings. He shooed the horses out of the trees and after a little hesitation they cantered away.

'Hey, don't you go getting any ideas, Lady,' he said.

The paint eyed him stoically, then went back to cropping the grass.

Brand stamped out the small cook fire, then went through the saddlebags and found little except some extra ammunition that he took and loaded into his own bags. He covered the bodies with the blankets, picked up the pair of handguns and packed them in his possibles bag, extra weapons were always handy. He had no use for the rifles so he propped them against the tree where Mennard's body rested. He had neither the time or the inclination to bury the bodies. He took the moment to reload his pistol.

Lady made an impatient sound. Brand leaned forward and stroked the paint's neck.

'Time we moved on.'

The sound of approaching, hard-ridden horses reached him. He guessed two of them. Coming his way. Friends of the pair he had just faced down? Here to relieve the watchers? Most likely having heard shooting. Bad timing for Brand them showing up now. The reason didn't really matter. Something told Brand the newcomers hadn't showed up to offer him the hand of friendship.

He mounted Lady and swung the paint out of the trees. As he moved into the open he saw a pair of riders cutting in his direction, bearing down on him. The thud of hooves mingled with the raised voice of one of the riders as he yanked a rifle from his saddle sheath.

Brand heard the shot. It missed by inches, the rider's aim off target because he was firing from a moving horse. Sawing Lady's reins about Brand moved her aside, the rifleman starting to line up for a second shot. Before he could do that his partner made his own move with the rope he had in his hands. He handled it with consummate skill, the coiled straightening out as he cast his throw. The loop settled over Brand's shoulders. He raised his arms to prevent it dropping further down his body, at the same time tightening Lady's reins to bring her to stop. Though the paint responded quickly, pulling herself to a halt, the rope tautened and Brand was dragged from the saddle. He felt himself falling and twisted his body, landing on his front. The impact was hard. Jolting him and knocking breath from his lungs. Dust billowed up from under his body. He fought against the momentary inaction, knowing that the rifleman would be making another play.

A rush of movement caught his attention. Brand swung his head around and caught a blurred image. The rifleman had left his saddle and was closing in fast. Brand saw a long shape in the man's hands. His rifle. It swung down at him. Brand threw up his arm to ward off the blow. It struck hard and drew a gasp from him. Pain burned along his arm. He heard the man mumble a curse. The rifle was pulled back for another strike.

Not again, Brand thought. *The hell with this . . .*

He let himself roll on his back. Swung out his left leg and hooked his booted foot around his attacker's ankle, then struck out with his own right foot. The blow was delivered with every ounce of force Brand could muster, the hard heel of his boot slamming into the man's knee. The knee collapsed, bone shattered, the leg bending against the ruined joint. A harsh scream burst from the man's lips as his limb gave way and he went down. On his hands and knees his face came level with Brand's and received the full force of Brand's follow-up kick. The crunch of the man's nose was followed by a flowering of blood. The man's head twisted to the side and he hit the ground moaning.

The rope around Brand began to tighten as it was pulled hard. He rolled on his left side and saw the source of the rope. A man on horseback, looping the trailing rope around his saddle horn, ready to drag Brand. Brand snatched his Colt free and took a fast shot at the rider. The shot went wild. So did his second as he was jerked around, but his third tore a furrow in the horse's left foreleg. The animal squealed and pulled sideways. The rider went for his own gun, letting go the rope, and returned a hasty shot that kicked up dirt feet short of Brand's prone body. It was the last mistake the man ever made. Letting go of the rope allowed it to slacken enough for Brand to set his aim. He triggered two more shots, fighting to keep his gun on target, and saw the rider fall back in his saddle, the .45 caliber slugs thumping into his chest. As the noose loosened from his shoulder Brand pushed to his knees, sensing movement behind him. He swiveled his body and saw the bloody-faced man half risen, despite his crippled leg and chest wounds, pulling his own revolver free. Brand didn't take time to think. He swept the Colt around, hammer already back, and put his last shot into the man's shoulder and he fell back.

Sucking air into his lungs Brand pushed to his feet, his fingers already working to punch out empty shell casings and reload the Colt. A noise alerted him but it was only Lady making herself known to him as she moved close.

'Not always about you,' Brand said, moving to stroke the paint's neck. Lady pushed her head against him. 'But hell, I know what you mean.'

He checked the chest shot man. He had slipped quietly from the saddle and lay on his back, staring up as Brand stood over him. The front of his dark shirt was wet with blood that was pulsing from the bullet wounds. A thin trickle ran from the corner of his slack mouth. Brand crouched beside him and felt the man's eyes turn to fix on him. He could hear the ragged sound of the man's labored breathing.

'Hell's teeth, son, you done turned that around on us.'

He was gray-haired, his gaunt face lined and creased as old leather. His clothing hung loosely on his skinny frame. Not a young man — and now not likely to get older — Brand figuring him to be desperate enough to take gun money.

'You made the choice when you took somebody's money.'

'Ain't about to be spending it now . . . hell's fire I should have stayed pushing cows . . . '

The man fell into a harsh coughing fit, bringing up more blood that coursed down his chin and dripped onto his shirt. He clutched at his chest.

Brand waited until the coughing ceased and the man settled.

'You feel like telling me who paid you?'

'It don't make any never mind now,' the man said. 'Big boss is a feller called Elias Bodine. Gang boss is Costigan. Made it sound all important we put anyone following us in the ground.' He managed a crooked smile. 'Looks as if I'll be there first.'

Elias Bodine.

It would be interesting to meet him face-to-face. Brand corrected himself. He *would* be meeting Bodine.

'You hear where this man hangs his hat?'

'Did pick up mention of Redigo is all.' He fumbled inside his blood-soaked shirt and pulled out a thick wad of banknotes. Held it up so Brand could see where one of his slugs had pierced the cash. Blood had turned the wad sodden. 'Try *The Blanco Palace*. If you catch up with him,' the man whispered, 'tell him I ain't giving him his blood money back.'

The hand dropped. The wad of notes

spilled across his chest, simply soaking up more of the dead man's blood.

Brand's left arm was starting to burn from being struck. He flexed his fingers. Moved his limb. At least it wasn't broken. He stood and crossed to where the other man lay.

'*Let me get my hand on a gun, you sonofabitch, and I'll finish you.*'

The man was hunched over, dripping blood from his crushed nose and favoring the leg Brand had smashed. His shoulder was a bloody mess as well. He was in no condition to do anything drastic. In his pained state he had even forgotten about the revolver on his hip. Brand bent over and slid it from the holster, throwing into the brush. He did the same with the fallen rifle.

'You'd leave a man with no damn gun?'

'I'm getting tired of you people making a fuss after you try to kill me. You expecting me to shake your hand?'

The man bent lower, cupping his bleeding face.

'It damnwell hurts.'

'Think of it as a lesson you learned the hard way.'

Without warning the man swept up his left hand. He had pulled a knife from inside his shirt and he lunged forward, sweeping the blade in at Brand's body. Brand arched his body away, the blade missing him by inches. The man grunted with the effort, making another sweep. This time Brand set himself and launched his booted foot in a roundhouse kick that caught the man across the side of his face, snapping his head back. The man uttered a low sigh, falling back, all effort gone from his body. He lay motionless, his neck twisted awkwardly and it didn't take too much guessing his neck was broken.

Brand turned away, cleared the trees and went to find Lady. She raised her head at Brand's approach, waiting while he gathered the reins and led her back to the trees. He tied the reins to a low branch, stroking the animal and praising her.

Then he went back to where the bodies lay, moving on to where their horses stood. He repeated what he had done with the first pair of mounts, stripping off saddles and removing the bridles and all the other trappings. He shooed the horses out of the trees and after a little hesitation they moved away.

Going to Lady, Brand loosened the reins and eased into the saddle. He turned the paint and found the trace left by the men he was trailing. In the scattering of hoof prints he made out the impression of the split shoe. He was still following the right trail.

Brand leaned forward and stroked the paint's neck.

'You did me a favor back there, Lady. Much obliged.'

The sky was shading over as daylight faded. Brand was going to need a place to sit out the night. He decided to keep riding for a while yet. Time left to choose a spot. Come morning he would pick up the trail again. The men he was trailing had been paid well to deter any pursuit. It made him realize the people behind the operation were bound and determined to remain undisturbed. Four men were dead and he had barely got into his stride.

If that was the way they wanted to play, Brand was just as set on stopping them. He accepted the way it was going to be. It did nothing to put him off. It was his job. Why he was here. And he refused to even consider backing down.

5

His name was Warren J. McCoy, forty odd years old and for eighteen of those years he had been a Texas Ranger, one of the small, elite band of lawmen who upheld the law in the vast region. It was a thankless task. Ill-paid, a Ranger was expected to provide his own clothing and spent much of his life in the saddle, crossing the trackless and hostile territory in pursuit of outlaws, Indians and as many types of criminals he could shake a stick at. A Ranger had to be determined, single-minded and content with his own company, and not expect too much in the way of praise at the end of it all.

McCoy was Texas born and bred. He hailed originally from Waco, though since his teen years when he left home and joined his first cattle drive, he had never been back home. Over the next long years he worked a number of jobs, but always at the forefront of his mind McCoy had a yearning to be a lawman. In his twenties he became a deputy in a small Texas town and he knew the moment he pinned on a badge he had found his true home. Over the next few years he had a number of posts as a lawman, never once having to draw his guns. At the first chance he got he applied for and eventually was accepted as a Texas Ranger. Whatever he might have been expecting, the truth was far from it.

On his first assignment, riding with a pair of experienced men, he got a taste of what wearing the badge could offer. That had been when a simple arrest had blown up into a bloody conflict. One of the men with him had been cut down with a shotgun blast that killed him outright and the second Ranger sustained a shoulder wound. McCoy had remained utterly calm throughout the whole affair. It never even crossed his mind he might be at risk. He saw what was happening and simply reacted. He had drawn one of the massive Walker Colts he carried and had put two .44 caliber slugs into the shooter, putting the man down in a heartbeat. In the aftermath McCoy had tended to his wounded colleague before riding back to the Ranger station with him, and with two dead men over their saddles.

With his credentials accepted McCoy made his name known within the ranks of the Rangers. He had a simple set of rules that saw him through any situation he had to face.

Give a man a choice. Surrender without a fight, or face the big pistols McCoy carried. He never asked twice and backing down wasn't in his makeup. McCoy's natural skill with his pair of Walker Colts became legendary. He carried no other type of handgun, just a Winchester 44–40 rifle in a sheath on his saddle. Despite the pistols' size and weight, some five pounds each, he handled the weapons with ease and alarming accuracy. Men had challenged him that the black powder and ball loading must have caused him problems, slowing his recharging and holding him back. McCoy had counted that both pistols loaded gave him twelve shots and that was enough to see him through any gunfight. His Ranger record proved his point. Over the long years McCoy's reputation preceded him and though a number of outlaws challenged him, and lost, others were all too ready to throw down their guns and raise their arms in the presence of Warren J. McCoy — Texas Ranger.

On that day the lean, hollow-cheeked man, thick, drooping mustache almost white and standing out against his brown skin, rode out of Handy and picked up the trail left by Jason Brand. They were near enough a day old but that made little difference to McCoy. Tracking was a big part of his job, so following Brand's trail was almost too easy.

He sat his big chestnut mare easy in his heavy Texas saddle, staring at the world from beneath the wide, curled brim of his black hat. He might have given the impression of indifference, yet in truth he missed nothing as he trailed casually from town, leaving Marshal Hicks staring after him.

'Tough one to figure out,' Toby Books said.

'That is one hard man,' Hicks said. 'I heard about Warren J. McCoy. Never lost a man he went after and brought in a lot over their saddles.'

'You see those pistols he's wearing? Biggest damn things I ever did see.'

'Walker Dragoon Colts. Forty-four caliber. Story goes if he has to draw them anyone facing him is a dead man.'

'Well,' Books said, 'I hope Mister Brand sees him coming.'

Hicks gave a chuckle. 'Don't you worry about Brand. He can handle someone like McCoy if he needs to.'

⋆　⋆　⋆

A few miles out of Handy, McCoy drew rein, slipping off the long black coat he was wearing. He folded the garment and tucked it under his blanket roll. The day was turning hotter than he had anticipated. Under the coat he wore a dark gray shirt and a neat, black string tie. He wore the double gun rig over black pants that were pulled over the high boots and spurs. Each holster, holding one of the large Dragoon Colts, was crafted in black leather and had rawhide thongs dangling ready to be tied down if needed. Over the left side pocket of his shirt McCoy wore the distinctive Texas Ranger silver badge — the star inside a circle — was so well known in the state that sometimes that was all it took to subdue a suspect.

Only now his wearing of the badge had become a mockery. McCoy was doing something for himself. In truth he was no longer an official Ranger. He had been dismissed from the Rangers after being caught out not only thieving, but also because he had betrayed the Ranger code and used his position to sell information. Although he had been forced to hand over his Texas Ranger badge, McCoy was still wearing one he had obtained for his personal use some years back. He still wore the badge because for the time being it would allow him to operate as if he was still part of the law force. By the time his deception was discovered he hoped to be a long way from Texas. Free and clear and with a sizable amount of money in his pocket.

Moving on McCoy drew the makings out of his shirt pocket and rolled a cigarette. He pulled a match and struck it with his thumbnail, lit the strong tobacco and drew deeply. He nudged the chestnut's sides and the horse moved off again.

'*Brand, I heard about you*,' McCoy said. 'Well, son, I'm coming and there ain't a damn thing you can do about it.'

THE CHASE

6

The isolated settlement of Blanco, Texas, lived up — *or down depending on personal views* — to its reputation. There was no kind of law in Blanco. It had its own rules and anyone visiting the place stuck to them. Those rules were pretty far-ranging in that a man stayed within them, or paid the price, which in Blanco's rule book was high. The place was a haven for those who strayed away from what would have been expected in a *civilized* society. Yet Blanco maintained its status within its own boundaries and tolerated *outsiders* as long as they didn't try to force themselves on the situation. Leave Blanco to its own business and any stranger would be safe unless he stepped out of line.

The town was a straggle of buildings either side of a main street that comprised dusty ruts and an uneven line. Buildings were untidy and poorly constructed. It wasn't so much that the constructions were false-fronted, more that the buildings were false-built. A mix of timber and adobe. Places to eat. Drink. Sleep if you weren't too fussy about cleanliness, or infestation. Which most of those passing through, whether for business or pleasure, weren't. A man on the owlhoot, or seeking temporary rest where it wouldn't cost too much, would choose Blanco because it asked no questions and made no judgments.

Blanco offered safety in numbers. Gave a modicum of protection to the lost and lonely, and perhaps a little relief in a life that had taken a turn for the worse.

As Brand took his horse along the street, picking up the sound of voices coming from saloons and eating houses, he could understand the attraction of Blanco for the solitary rider. The security, albeit, brief and not without risk would be welcome to someone needing company. He spent time enough himself on lonely trails, moving from place to place in the course of his business. The need for the sound of a human voice, the presence of another person, they were welcome distractions and not to be passed over lightly.

He saw the crudely painted, garish sign that told him he had found *The Blanco Palace*. A wry smile edged his lips as he looked the place over. It was a long way from anything resembling a palace. A two-story, timber structure with windows either side of the batwing doors on the ground floor. Despite it only being mid-morning the noise coming from the saloon suggested business started early. Brand hitched Lady to the rail alongside other horses. With his dusty clothes and unshaven face he would pass as acceptable. He slipped the loop off the holstered Colt and made his way to the entrance, feeling the boardwalk move underfoot.

As he pushed through the batwings the noise and the ambience seemed to reach out and wrap itself around him. As did the smell of unwashed bodies, tobacco smoke and fried food that rose in his nostrils. Brand let the doors close behind him as he scanned the saloon. Most of the tables were occupied. Customers were drinking, others eating. At one end of the long bar a large, steaming urn provided coffee, while a couple of aproned men served drinks. From an open door next to the bar the smell of cooking meat filled the air. The whole place seethed with humanity. A staircase led to the upper floor where unpainted doors led to a number of rooms. *The Blanco Palace* might not have much else going for it but what it did offer it did with a certain enthusiasm.

No one turned to stare at Brand as he eased his way across the sawdusted floor. He made his way to the bar, spotting a gap in the line of men bellied up to it. It took him a minute or two before he caught the eye of one the aproned tenders.

'Beer?' Brand said.

The man took a glass and turned to one of the heavy casks mounted on a sawhorse behind him. Brand watch as the man opened the spigot and allowed amber liquid to fill the glass. He brought the foam-topped glass and slid it across to Brand. He slid coins across the bar and picked up the glass. The beer was warm but it went down Brand's dry throat easily.

'Look like you needed that,' the bartender said.

'Long ride,' Brand said.

'New in Blanco?'

'Got in a couple of minutes ago.' Brand glanced around the saloon. 'Lively crowd you got.'

The bartender smiled. 'Hell, you should see 'em when they really open up.' He was a lean, pale-faced man, losing his hair. 'Passing through, or going to stay a while?'

'Haven't made up my mind yet.' Brand pointed at the open door where the cooking smell was coming from. 'The food as good as it smells?'

'Way to find out is to try it.'

Brand sank half the glass of beer. 'Can I get a steak with all the trimmings?'

'You can have what you want as long as you pay for it.'

It had just come to Brand that he was hungry and staying around *The Blanco Palace* would allow him to do some quiet observing. He asked the price of a meal, paid for it and took his beer with him to an empty table. It was near the back wall and allowed him a clear view of the saloon.

A half dozen women were drifting in and out of the tables, stopping to talk to customers, some of them taking a seat and having drinks bought for them. Brand saw a couple lead men upstairs and vanish into the rooms. The saloon offered more than a drink and food.

He was still nursing his beer when a shadow slid across his table. When he glanced up he saw a smiling face looking down at him. The girl, which she was, had a powdered face and chestnut hair. Still attractive though Brand wondered how long she would retain her youthful appearance. The thin dress she wore revealed almost as much as it covered.

'Company?'

Brand was about to say no, but changed his mind. Saloon girls, apart from their expected functions, were a good source of information. They spent their time in and around the customers and had a habit of picking up information.

'Why not,' he said.

The girl slipped easily onto the chair next to his. He caught a whiff of the cheap perfume she was wearing.

'I got food coming,' he said, 'but we can talk while I eat.'

'I'm Lydia. What do I call you?'

Brand had worked on a name to use while he was in Blanco. Assuming an identity was a simple enough way of hiding who he really was. He couldn't conceal his looks, apart from being unshaven, so that was something he had to take a chance on.

'Jack Boyd.'

'Will Jack Boyd buy me a drink?'

Brand took money from his pocket and slid it across the table.

'Whatever you want and I'll have another beer.'

Lydia scooped up the money. 'Don't rush away, Jack.'

She made her way to the bar and Brand took his time looking over the busy saloon again. At a table in the center of the floor he spotted a man who seemed to be showing some interest. When he saw Brand looking his way the man averted his eyes.

Okay, friend, Brand decided, *you had your look. Now let's see if anything comes of it.*

Brand's food arrived, with Lydia not far behind. She placed their drinks on the table, casting her gaze over the steak and trimmings.

'Hope you have a good appetite,' she said.

Brand tackled the food, finding the

steak tender and juicy. He caught a glimpse of Lydia watching him, a smile on her face.

'I like to see a man enjoying his food,' she said. She raised her glass and took a sip, frowning slightly.

'Drink not so good?'

'I still don't have much of a taste for liquor.'

'How long you been here in Blanco?'

'Does it show that much?'

'Some.'

'A girl has to earn a living.'

'How did you end up in Blanco?'

'I fell for a man who decided he didn't want to work for a living. He figured that stealing was a fast way to earn money. Trouble was he didn't do it very well. So we ran out of money and just drifted, down the social ladder the further we went. We ended up here and then he got himself shot by someone faster when he got caught cheating. I had no money to travel further so here I am.' She studied him. 'Now you ask a lot of questions, Jack Boyd.'

'I guess so. Here's another one. The feller in the bright blue shirt over to the table across from us. You know him?'

Lydia took a cautious glance, then looked back at Brand.

'Stay away from him, Jack. That's Lige Costigan. Pay him enough and he'd shoot the President himself. Everybody in Blanco knows to stay away from Costigan. He runs with a bad crowd.' She reached out and gripped Brand's wrist. 'Hey, are you listening to me? Don't cross Costigan.'

Brand finished his meal and sat back. He saw that Costigan kept looking his way, then leaning forward to speak with the two men sitting at the table. As Brand drained his beer he saw Costigan's two companions push back their chairs and make their way out of the saloon. Costigan sat back, rolling himself a cigarette, a faint smile on his face, as if he had a secret he was keeping to himself.

'I need to check something out,' he said to Lydia.

'Remember what I said.'

'I will.'

Brand walked casually out the saloon, pausing as he pushed his way through the swing doors. He had left Lady at the hitch post. Now she was gone. He cast around and saw in the distance the two men who had left the saloon. They were already clear of the edge of Blanco, leading Lady by the reins and heading for a ragged bunch of outbuildings and a sagging stable. Brand stepped off the walk and made his way along the street.

He saw one of the men lead Lady into the stable. The other man vanished from sight inside a shack, leaving the area deserted. He wondered what the men were playing at, obviously following some order Costigan had given them. Brand slipped the Colt from his holster and thumbed in a sixth cartridge before he dropped it back. His instinct was nudging him towards thinking he was going to need every bullet he had. If this was a game Costigan had initiated Brand had no intention of coming out the loser.

The whole thing had the smell of a setup and a pretty amateurish one. Taking a man's horse was bound and determined to get a result. It had. Only Brand was no tenderfoot liable to go blundering in without assessing the odds.

When he got to within thirty feet of the shack, with the stable another fifteen away, Brand slowed his walk. He caught a hurried glimpse of someone moving from a side door of the stable and easing into the shadows behind the shack. If this was a setup it was pretty blatant.

7

Brand had a feeling of disquiet as he closed in on the shack. On the fringes of his hearing were the normal sounds coming from Blanco's main street, now a distance behind him. Too far away to be fully heard but making an impression on his senses. His right hand hovered over the butt of his holstered Colt. He stared around the edges of the shack, eyes probing the area, searching. He trusted his senses. Allowed them to dictate his intentions, but right now he couldn't decide whether this was instinct or overriding caution. His fingers had started to curl around the Colt. Gripping the butt to lift the weapon.

And then he picked up the soft, dry creak of a hinge, his eyes flickering in the direction of the shack's closed door. He caught movement. Slight, but enough to draw his full attention. The door eased open a few inches. Slowly and followed by the blued metal of a shotgun's double barrels poking into view. In that same moment Brand saw a shadow emerge from the far corner of the shack and start to enlarge as the owner stepped forward. The hot near-silence was interrupted by the unmistakable sound of the shotgun's double hammers being cocked. The sound threw a chill over him; there was something cold and alarming at the prospect of being hit by a shotgun charge; Brand had witnessed the effects from such a weapon and he understood the imagery that sprang to mind. The door began to swing wider. His suspicion of being set up was proving correct and Brand knew his time was running out fast. Too damn fast. And he had two to deal with now. The shotgunner was closest . . .

So deal with him first and hope the other man didn't have a shotgun as well.

Brand moved fast, the Colt slipping

from the holster in a smooth and easy motion, hammer already eased back as he drew. He dropped to a semi-crouch, turning the muzzle towards the ever-widening door and judged where the hidden shooter would be standing behind the flimsy wooden wall. He saw the shotgun muzzle poke further into view, starting to angle in his direction.

And out of the corner of his eye he saw the distant shadow of the second shooter merging into the shape of a man holding a handgun. Even as that was registering, Brand was triggering the Colt, placing his opening shot into the shack wall and close to the doorframe. He followed with three more, close-spaced, and fired as he held back the trigger and heeled the hammer. The hard roll of shots sounded loud. Brand saw wood splinters explode from the wall as his .45 slugs pounded the timber. Holes appeared. The door was pushed back as the shotgunner fell into view, bloody holes in his body. His heavy bulk hitting the door and sliding along it, his weapon dropping from loose fingers . . .

. . . and by then Brand had dropped into a lower crouch, seeing the man with the handgun stepping clear of the shack's corner, the muzzle of his revolver already on target.

The thunder of a shot came from behind Brand. Close enough to ring in his ears and he swore he felt the breath of it passing. It hit the would-be shooter high in the chest, on the left. The power of the shot twisted the man around as a gout of bloody debris blew out his back on his way down. The man hit the ground on his front, face slamming into the surface with force enough to crush his nose and dislocate his jaw. The sound of the shot was still fading as Brand turned his head and saw the dark outline of the shooter through the cloud of powder smoke wreathed around him. The smoke came from the barrel of a big .44 caliber Walker Dragoon Colt the man held in a sinewy fist.

'Came close,' the man said.

Brand eyed the lean, dark clad figure, noting the gleaming badge pinned to his shirt and the twin holsters around his waist. He was shucking empty casings from his Colt as he took all this in, quickly reloading the .45.

'Grateful you showed up when you did,' he said. 'These boys play rough.'

The man stroked fingers through the generous moustache adorning his upper lip.

'Warren J. McCoy,' he said. He spoke as if the name meant something. 'And you'd be Jason Brand.'

'Hell of a way to get introduced. Grateful you showed up when you did,' he said. 'These boys play rough.'

'We need to talk about this.'

'After I deal with something first.'

He collected Lady from the stable and led her back along the dusty, rutted street. He was heading back to the saloon where Lige Costigan had spoken to his partners before sending them to draw Brand out.

McCoy fell in behind him. Not crowding Brand but indicating his presence.

As he walked in the direction of the saloon he wasn't slow to notice the lack of interest in the shooting. Blanco was living up to its reputation as a no-nonsense place where gunfire was the norm and not likely to interest anyone. The population might eventually stir into action if the place became *too* quiet.

Brand settled Lady at the hitch rail outside *The Blanco Palace*, stepping up on the boardwalk. Brand moved by a loose group of men by the entrance. Their glances were not entirely friendly but that was as far as it went.

He pushed through the swing doors and into the saloon. It was still as noisy. Still crowded. Lige Costigan still sat at the same table, only now he was facing the door, and when he saw Brand the anticipation on his face turned to surprise. He had been expecting his friends — not the man they had gone to ambush.

Costigan rose, kicking his chair back, his right hand dropping to the weapon holstered on his hip. The space between Costigan and Brand cleared, leaving a clear path as they faced off. No more than a few seconds had passed. The saloon was suddenly silent. Brand kept moving forward, no hesitation as he drew the Colt, cocked and fired in a single motion, Costigan's slower action leaving his own revolver still only half-drawn. The .45 slug hit him in the right shoulder, shattering the collar bone. The impact spun Costigan round in a half circle. He got caught up in a chair and went to the floor in a clumsy fall.

Brand moved to stand over him, reaching down to snatch the man's revolver from the holster and tuck it in his belt. He grasped hold of Costigan's blue shirt and rolled the man over onto his back. He ignore the ragged moans coming from Costigan.

'*Son of a bitch*,' Costigan said through clenched teeth.

He clamped his left hand over the wound in his shoulder, blood quickly seeping between his fingers. His face had already turned pale and sweat glistened on his flesh.

'You should choose better partners,' Brand said. 'That pair out there were pretty useless. You must have hired them from the same place you got Lander and Mennard and those other hardcases.'

'*Damn* . . . '

'You boys give outlaws a bad name.'

Brand glanced around the still silent saloon, briefly wondering why it was still quiet. Then he spotted McCoy standing in the doorway, both his Colt Dragoons in his hands, covering the crowd.

'There any kind of doctor in this excuse for a town?' the Ranger said.

'Philo Dunmore is the closest we got to that,' someone said. 'Doctors horses as well as people.'

'Somebody go fetch him,' McCoy snapped.

He stood with his back to the wall, eyes scanning the big room and daring anyone to go against him. When one of the men broke from the crowd and scuttled to the door McCoy halted him with one of the gun barrels.

'You come back with anything 'cept this Dunmore feller, boy, I don't rate your chances of seeing tomorrow morning.'

The man offered a cheesy smile. 'No problem, Ranger.'

By this time Brand had hauled Costigan off the floor and propped him up on a chair.

'What you boys have in numbers you lose in quality,' he said softly to the moaning man. 'Way you're going, Costigan, you're earning your pay the hard way. Now you're up to your neck in trouble.'

'You could be dead if you mess with me. Could get you killed . . . '

'You forgot already that's what you sent your partners to do? I could pull this trigger and worry later. Either way, Costigan, you're out of luck. Ranger back there isn't going to let you walk away even if I do.'

'I got friends. Powerful friends.'

'They powerful enough to stop a bullet right now? I don't see them around.'

McCoy had edged further into the saloon, his extended Walker Colts in plain sight.

'Costigan, don't figure on your *powerful* friends covering your ass,' McCoy said. 'Like the man says they ain't liable to be showing up anytime soon. Son, you are nigh on in a lonesome place. It's time to protect your own skin. Way you're going right now I can see a cell in Huntsville with your name on it . . . '

'I got a name for you, Costigan,' Brand said, '*Elias Bodine*.'

He was watching Costigan for a reaction. And got one as he saw the man's eyes go wide with surprise.

'Don't know the name,' he said hurriedly.

The tone in his voice betrayed him.

'The hell you don't. Same as you

don't know where I'd find him. Like Redigo.'

McCoy had spotted the reaction.

'I say we drag this worthless piece of a turd out of here and put him in a cell,' he said.

Someone in the crowd of spectators laughed. 'That's going to be worth seeing, Ranger.'

'Yeah, be interesting seeing as we don't have no cells in Blanco.'

'Or a damn jail.'

'And there ain't any law in town neither.'

That brought more laughter.

'There is as long as I'm here,' McCoy said. 'You people step away.' He brandished his revolvers. 'Ranger law and I'll use it on any man who steps out of line. Name's Warren J. McCoy and I'll warrant it's one some of you boys have heard before. I'll brook no resistance and you know what will happen if you go against a Texas Ranger.'

8

'Only one of you,' a voice called from the back of the room. 'What do think about that?'

'Not a great deal coming from a man who stands in the shadow. Step out and face me.'

There was no response to that.

Before anything else happened two men came into the saloon. One was the man who had stepped out earlier. With him was a skinny individual carrying a battered leather bag. He had a harried look to him, as if all of life was a worry and he was carrying most of it on his boney shoulders. He wore baggy dark pants tucked into mule-ear boots and a crumpled off-white shirt under a stained vest.

'You Dunmore?' Brand asked.

'Yeah.'

'Then I got a patient for you. One of

the two legged kind.'

Brand moved aside so Dunmore could see Lige Costigan. The doctor peered at Costigan, seeing the blood, and shook his head. He made a visual inspection of Costigan's shoulder, clucking to himself.

'Bullet's still in there. Nothin' I can do here,' he said. 'Have to move him down to my office.' He glanced across at McCoy, fidgeting uncomfortably. 'No one told me a Ranger was involved.'

'You done something wrong?' McCoy asked.

Dunmore cleared his throat. '*Nooo*,' he said, drawing out the single word.

'Don't worry about him,' Brand said. '*I* shot Costigan.'

Dunmore seemed mollified at that. He looked around the saloon. 'Couple of you people help this man down to my place.'

With Costigan gone the tension in the saloon eased off. Although there were still hostile glares Brand and McCoy were generally ignored. Brand led the way outside. The Ranger didn't holster his guns until they were clear.

'Eating house along the street,' Brand said. 'Don't know about you but I could favor a cup of coffee.'

'Sounds about right.'

★ ★ ★

The eating house was cool and shadowed from the hot Texas sun. Brand and McCoy took a table facing the door and kitchen. The waitress, a rawboned woman in her forties with a white apron over a loose gingham dress wandered over. They ordered coffee, waited until the steaming mugs had been delivered before either of them spoke.

'Elias Bodine,' McCoy said as a conversation opener.

'The name isn't new to you?'

'We on a share by share basis here?'

Brand tasted his coffee. Found it strong and full of flavor.

'Who is he?' Brand said, playing cautious.

'A man with influence. Important friends. Money and lots of it.' McCoy paused to drink. 'And secrets . . . '

'You after him?'

'Yes, and I intend to bring him down.'

'He wanted for a crime?'

'Having a hell of a time proving it but I will see that sonofabitch in chains before I quit.' McCoy leaned back in the hard chair. 'Your turn.'

'My assignment is to locate the men who hit that train in Handy and took something away.'

'Has to be more than a pile of money. You going to tell me what?'

'There were two Pinkerton agents on that train. They were bringing evidence to Washington that would name names and present documented evidence concerning a group involved in high level corruption. Those involved include businessmen, politicians, bankers. Members of the legal profession. Even military personnel. Signed and witnessed testimony. People willing to point the finger. If that evidence reached the appropriate quarters a lot of people are going to have a difficult time.'

'Evidence like that would cause a lot of upset. And those involved would be desperate to make sure it didn't get to Washington.'

'Like Elias Bodine?'

McCoy nodded. 'These people have the money and the contacts to send out their hired guns to take that evidence and stop it being aired.'

'There are names on the lists that identify witnesses ready to talk. Witnesses who would need to be silenced.' Brand signaled the waitress for more coffee. 'What's Bodine's connection?'

'I been investigating him since a man named Walt Coltrane was found shot in alley in El Paso a few months back. Coltrane was a Ranger working under-cover. I knew him. Spoke to him in hospital before he died. He told me it was Bodine who had him attacked because he'd found out Bodine was in league with some big-named individu-als. He'd overheard a conversation that hinted at corruption and something about evidence having been collected. Got me curious so I started tracking Bodine and his *friends*. Found out the man had been associating with some lowdown characters. Men who hired out their guns with no questions asked. Men like Dane Mennard. Vince Lander. Costigan was involved as well.'

'Seems likely we're on a close trail pointing towards Redigo,' Brand said.

'Don't it just.'

'Maybe warrants a ride there. I'm getting the feeling we might find something of interest.'

McCoy raised his cup of coffee. 'I suggest we get ourselves something to eat 'fore we move on. Fair piece to Redigo. Wouldn't like to make it on an empty belly.'

'You know this part of the country?'

'Most of it.'

'What about Little Creek?'

'Rode through from time to time. Has a spurline. Telegraph.'

'The two things I'm interested in,'

Brand said. 'You go ahead and eat. I just finished a meal myself back in the saloon so I'm fine.'

Brand left McCoy to his meal and went to check on Lady.

* * *

McCoy ate slowly, working things over in his mind. He had plenty to think about. He felt certain he had convinced Brand he was still a legitimate Ranger, and with that established the man would be freer with his talk. Being at Brand's side meant McCoy could keep the man in his sight. He found it hard not to smile when he recalled what he had told Brand about Walt Coltrane. The man had been shot. In the back. It had been McCoy who had fired the gun. A backup .44–40 Colt so that he hadn't needed to use his Walkers. And yes, he had spoken to the man on his deathbed, expressing concern over the undercover Ranger's injury, with Coltrane not even suspecting it had been

McCoy who had done the shooting. If Coltrane had not been getting too close he might have lived, but part of McCoy's deal with Bodine was to divert any untoward interest.

Now McCoy had Brand's ear and if it became possible the man might lead McCoy to Henry Quinlan all the better. Which was why McCoy needed to keep the man alive — until his usefulness came to an end.

McCoy ate his meal, finished with more coffee, then paid and made his way to where Brand was waiting.

★ ★ ★

They rode out of Blanco an hour later and by evening they were able to see the small town of Little Creek from the higher ground. Lamps were being lit against the encroaching darkness.

A straggle of buildings. Smoke rising from chimneys. Cattle pens and sheds. The curving shine of steel rails. There was a small depot. The soft gleam of the meandering creek that gave the place its name. They rode downslope and entered Little Creek after cutting through a copse of trees and brush, swinging across the small bridge that straddled the water course. The discordant jangle of an out-of-tune piano came from a saloon they passed. The few people moving about paid them little attention.

McCoy drew rein outside a stone and adobe building that declared itself as the town's law office.

'Jim Pine is Marshal,' the Ranger informed Brand.

'I know Pine,' Brand said as he tethered the paint.

They stretched the kinks out of their bones before they stepped up on the boardwalk. McCoy pushed open the heavy timber door and they went inside.

The figure behind the oak desk glanced up, his brown face clean shaven and breaking into a welcoming smile as he recognized both his visitors.

It was a tense moment for McCoy, waiting to see Pine's reaction to him.

He knew he was taking a risk showing himself here, but the end result would be worth the risk if it brought McCoy what he needed.

'Ain't seen you for a while, W.J. Hell, we don't get much from the outside world down here in this godforsaken place,' he said in a slow, measured tone. He stood and reached out to take McCoy's hand, then widened his smile as he offered the hand to Brand. 'And a damn long time since I seen you, Jason.'

Pine was a tall, lean figure, his youthful appearance concealing his middle age. He dressed plain and dark, only the shine of his badge relieving his sober dress. He wore a .45 caliber Peacemaker on his left hip, butt forward and angled for ease of draw. He had a reputation as a steady lawman. Slow to anger but when the need arose he was no slouch with the pistol he carried.

McCoy had crossed to the hot stove where a coffee pot sat gently steaming. He picked mugs from the hooks on the wall and filled three, passing them out to Brand and Pine.

'Never see him for months,' Pine said, 'then in he walks and treats the place like home.'

'How long *you* been calling Little Creek home?' Brand asked.

'Couple years now. Suits me nicely after the Nueces Strip. Man, that was a hell of a place. You'd know, W.J.'

McCoy nodded. The Nueces Strip had a reputation from lawlessness and was known as a haven for smugglers. The Texas Rangers were often involved on the strip of land.

'Been quiet for a while,' he said.

'Now I know you ain't been around much,' Pine said to Brand. 'Then I did hear you kind of slipped off the map. Then I learned you were working for some Justice Department outfit.'

'Keeps me busy,' Brand said and left it at that.

'Fine,' Pine said. 'So what brings you two to Little Creek? I miss something?'

'Few days back there was a holdup in Handy,' Brand said. 'People died and an item taken. Gang headed south. In this direction. I have an idea they might have caught a train here heading for Redigo.'

'Last train from here was two days ago. You fellers are in luck. Next one out goes in the morning.' Pine glanced at McCoy. 'Rangers involved too?'

McCoy nodded. 'There's a connection between Brand's business and a Ranger investigation. Kind of ties us close.'

Pine smiled. 'Nice to see law working together,' he said, a faint mocking tone to his words.

'What time does the train pull out, Jim?' Brand asked.

'Six-thirty on the dot.'

'There someplace I can get a hot bath and a shave?' Brand asked. 'Telegraph office and a good livery to rest the horses?'

Pine gave them directions. Brand and McCoy saw to their horses first, then took themselves over to the telegraph which was located at the rail depot.

Brand wrote his message and sent it off. Any reply was to be delivered to Pine's office.

At the bathhouse they had their clothes brushed down while they soaked in big wooden tubs, cleaning off the accumulated trail dust. When they were dressed Brand stepped next door and relaxed in a chair while he was shaved. Feeling cleaner he made his way back to the jail. McCoy was already there, sampling more of Pine's coffee. Brand took a cup and stretched out in a wooden chair.

'Jim's on his rounds,' McCoy offered. He indicated a buff envelope on the desk. 'Came for you just 'fore you walked in.'

Brand opened the telegram and read the short, to the point, message from McCord.

Stay with it. Will keep you appraised any developments when you reach Redigo. Play your hand close. Some information says Quinlan could be heading for Redigo. There is a wild card in play. McCoy is not on official duty. He's been dismissed as a Ranger. McCord.

'Anything helpful?' McCoy asked.

'Nothing I didn't know already. Just telling me I was right.'

Brand folded the message and put it in his shirt pocket, securing the button. He took up his coffee and drank, casually eyeing McCoy across the rim of his cup.

A wild card in play.

If McCoy was no longer a Ranger, what was the masquerade for? The logical answer was McCoy being in league with the people Brand was searching for. Which meant Brand was going to have to stay on the alert.

* * *

The train showed up on time. It comprised a noisy locomotive, two passenger coaches, a box car that held freight and a section for horses. At the rear was a caboose. Brand and McCoy

125

got their horses settled, then found seats on one of the coaches. They had spent the night in the jail, using the cots in the empty cells and Pine woke them in the early hours so they could meet the train when it pulled in.

'Don't make it so long next time,' Pine said before they left. 'Hope you find who you're looking for.'

'We will,' Brand said, and thought he might not like what he found.

It was beginning to show light as the train pulled out, amid a great deal of noise and steam. Black smoke billowed from the stack. Brand felt the coach shudder and vibrate under him. He tried to settle in the hard seat. Across from him McCoy simply leaned back, staring out the dusty window, seemingly out of anything to say.

Brand was trying to figure the man's part in the affair. On the surface McCoy seemed to be what he was portraying. A dedicated Texas Ranger, on the hunt. But now he had received McCord's suggestion he had a *wild card* close, Brand had to wonder just where McCoy fitted into the picture.

Brand grumbled inwardly. This assignment had already thrown up a number of obstacles, so Brand did not need any other problems. He also knew he had no choice in the matter. All he could do was keep his eyes and ears open, stay sharp, and make sure he was ready when — *not if* — things turned against him.

It wouldn't be the first time that had happened, and God willing he survived, it most likely wouldn't be the last.

9

Right at that moment Elias Bodine was in a foul mood. Mainly caused by the fact one of his minions had reported seeing W. J. McCoy in Redigo. The Ranger had been spotted in one of the saloons on main street. And he had been with a man who fit the description of the man known as Jason Brand.

'What the hell is McCoy playing at?' Bodine wanted to know.

'He should have disposed of Brand by now. Left his body to rot out somewhere away from town.'

Across the hotel suite, relaxing in one of the fat leather armchairs, Jay Bledsoe sat forward.

'I suggest he has his reasons,' he said in that quiet way he had.

Bledsoe, a lean, sharp-eyed man, wore a black suit with a starched white shirt and a lace strip down the front.

The effect gave him the appearance of an effete fop, but it was far from the truth. His refined look was disturbed by the cold, expressionless look in his pale, almost reptilian eyes. Bledsoe earned his way by being one of the most effective and remorseless gunmen Bodine had ever encountered. Bodine employed him as his personal bodyguard, paying him well and for that he received the man's full attention.

Around his slim hips Bledsoe wore a black leather belt and holster. It rode high on his hip, the supple leather holster holding a short-barreled Colt's Peacemaker, nickel plated, with grained walnut grips. Before having the revolver plated Bledsoe had asked for the front sight to be removed and the barrel made smooth. It was no affectation. Bledsoe had witnessed more than one man shot down because a snagging front sight had slowed a quick draw and given an opponent that split-second advantage. He didn't cast himself as a fast-draw expert. Simply a man who pulled his gun and took his moment to aim, rather than fire before he had a sound target. Nor did he ascribe to the posturing and bravado of others who liked their moment of glory, especially if they had an audience. Jay Bledsoe, once he had committed himself to a shootout, drew his gun and placed his shot, taking no pleasure in the act. Those who knew him as well as any could understood his manner and gave him the respect his skill offered him.

'Tell me what you mean,' Bodine said.

'Our doughty ex-Ranger has sold his soul for money,' Bledsoe explained. 'He did it because he was close to coming up to retirement from the Rangers and when he did he'd be just another unemployed man with a gun, years of experience tracking criminals, and little to show for all those dedicated years as a lawman. He'd be destined to walk away from the Rangers with nothing but the clothes he wears, his guns and his horse. Not much to show for all those years. McCoy is no fool. He doesn't want to end his time as a penniless drifter. Which is why he took your offer. One last hunt that will hand him a sizeable amount of money. Enough for him to spend his final years in relative comfort.'

Bodine stood and crossed the room, helping himself to a tumbler of whisky. He showed the bottle to Bledsoe, who shook his head.

'You should know by now, Mister Bodine. I never drink when I'm working.' He offered a thin smile. 'Oh, it might not look as if I'm working right now, but I am. Looking after you. I just make it look easy.'

'So . . . *McCoy?*'

'Right now he's staying close to Brand, because Brand is tracking the ones who carried out the robbery. And we don't know that Brand might also have other things on his mind.'

'*Quinlan?*'

'Our intrepid investigator. The man who compiled the documents that have you and all those other members of your little group. We both know if those documents he collected get into the hands of Senator Beauchamp, Washington is going to have a field day hauling you all in for conspiracy. Fraud. Blackmail. Crooked dealings on government contracts . . .' Bledsoe said. 'Oh . . . and a few cases of murder. Have I missed anything?'

Bodine swallowed his whisky and poured a second.

'Just confirm, Bledsoe, you *are* working on my side? Just then you sounded like a prosecutor outlining his case.'

'I'm on your side, Mister Bodine. Simply pointing out the parameters of what we're facing.'

Bodine made a sound deep in his throat. 'Comforting that you actually said what *we're* facing. Not just what *I'm* facing.'

'Mister Bodine, you pay, I play. You have my word.'

10

The more Brand thought about it the stronger his suspicion became. There was nothing tangible he could put his finger on but he couldn't shake off the nagging feeling where McCoy was concerned. He tried to push the thoughts out of his mind. All he succeeded in doing was making them persist. He realized that if he let them grow he was going to lose sight of why he was here in Redigo.

He stood at the hotel room's window, fastening his shirt, watching the traffic moving back and forth and concentrated on the matter at hand.

He needed to find Henry Quinlan. The man was an important piece of the puzzle. The one that could connect Brand to the people behind this whole affair. If Quinlan had come here, to Redigo, because he had some plan to get his hands back on the case of documents things could turn nasty very quickly.

He finished dressing, pulling on the shoulder holster and slipping the adapted Colt into place. He strapped on his regular revolver, checking the full load before settling the weapon. The dark suit jacket concealed the shoulder rig. Brand set the wide brimmed hat, left the room and locked the door. Downstairs he handed his key over, then strolled along the boardwalk in the direction of the telegraph office, which was at the far end of the street.

'I was waiting for my assistant to come back,' the operator said. 'Got a couple of messages for you, Mister Brand.'

He passed over the envelopes and Brand stood by the window as he read them. Both were from McCord and they confirmed Brand's concerns.

McCoy is dangerous.

The second message simply added further information. *Senator Eugene*

134

Beauchamp has found the man who gave out the information about the Pinkertons. He worked in Beauchamp's employ. He was paid to leak the whereabouts of the two detectives. McCoy's name came up again. Contact with Rangers shows McCoy has no morals when it comes to killing anyone who gets in his way. If you come in contact handle it. McCord.

'Any replies, Mister Brand?'

Brand shook his head. 'Not yet. Thanks.'

He left the office and paused to light a fresh cigar. He felt a dry wind drifting along the street, raising pale dust.

He failed to prevent McCoy's name from intruding on his thoughts.

Knowing what he did about the man raised doubts in Brand's mind.

What was McCoy up to?

His current evasiveness couldn't be good.

Come to think about it Brand realized he hadn't seen the man for a while. McCoy had said something about doing some local checking of his own and Brand had no hold on the man to stop him doing that.

He just wondered just what the man was up to.

McCoy.

Now Bodine.

Quinlan.

All connected. He needed to bring those connections together.

That, though he had no idea, was going to happen very quickly and he would be standing right in the middle of it all.

11

The alley was dark and littered with trash. It gave off a sour smell. The two men waiting in the shadows were congratulating themselves on having fallen lucky, being offered a large amount of cash for a few minutes' work. Half had already been paid. They would claim the rest when their victim was dead. They had been waiting for the man they knew as Brand to leave the telegraph office. He had been well described to them, so when the tall figure appeared they had no trouble identifying him.

'Going to be easy,' the one called Morgan said.

'Big feller,' Brandt said.

Morgan chuckled. 'He'll have further to fall then.'

They pressed against the wall, waiting. Watching Brand as he moved in their direction.

'Soon as he gets level you grab his arm and pull him in the alley.'

Brandt nodded. He was the bigger of the two, broad across his shoulders.

They heard the steady sound of footsteps. Brand's shadow fell across the mouth of the alley. Morgan stepped back to give his partner room. As Brand crossed the opening Brandt lunged, big hands reaching to grab at Brand's shirt. He got a solid grip, braced himself and yanked Brand sideways, dragging him off the boardwalk and into the alley.

'*Yeah*,' Morgan breathed, '*here's something for you*, bucko.'

The hickory club, Morgan's favorite weapon, swung around, clouting Brand across the back of his head. The brim of his hat cushioned some of the force, but there was still enough to make him stumble.

Morgan grunted. Swung the club a second time with increased force. It slammed across the side of Brand's head and he went down to the ground.

Morgan stepped back, the wooden

club still clutched in his hand.

'Didn't think he was going down.'

His partner, Brandt, grinned. 'Well he did, so let's make sure he don't get up again.'

'Yeah. Sooner we get her done sooner we can get our hands on the rest of that money.'

'Be nice to have some for a change.'

'Hey, maybe this son of a bitch has some in his pockets.'

'Well, he ain't going to be needing it where he's going.'

'Just turn him over.'

Brandt bent over the motionless figure sprawled on the ground. He caught hold of Brand's coat and heaved him over, ready to start using his club again.

He saw the open eyes staring up at him. The bright streak of blood coursing down the face. And then he saw the round, black muzzle of the cut-down Colt in Brand's fist, the weapon jutting forward. Brandt started a yell that didn't come. There was a bright flash. A stunning blow as the .45 caliber slug struck, tearing in through his face and angling up into his brain. Brandt fell back, unaware of the large chunk of skull separating as the mushrooming slug exited in a burst of red and gray.

Morgan saw the moment and felt a sickness in his stomach. The grisly sight etched in his mind and it held him motionless. It was that paralysis that was his undoing. He failed to see Brand's hand move. Failed to see the Colt move and find a second target. The pistol fired and the slug thudded into Morgan's left thigh. Pain followed seconds later. A terrible burst of agony as the lead slug cleaved flesh and shattered bone. Morgan went down, a shocked gasp bursting from his lips. He let go the club and clutched at his crippled limb, feeling blood starting to bubble from the wound. Then he was on the ground, experiencing pain worse than anything he had ever known.

Brand climbed slowly to his feet, left

hand reaching up to press against his head.

Damn but it hurt.

He stood there, swaying slightly as his senses realigned themselves. If Morgan's blow had been a few inches higher, contacting with his skull, the outcome would have been different. Brand had taken blows to his skull on other occasions — too many — and they invariably produced drastic results. Not that he wasn't suffering from this particular hit and the clout to the side of his face had left a nasty, stinging gash that was bleeding freely. But at least he was back on his feet.

He picked up a harsh, hurt sound. It came from Morgan, writhing about in the dust, hugging his damaged leg.

Brand crouched beside the man, Morgan's eyes fixing on him.

'No more money,' Brand said. 'You don't get paid if you mess up.'

Morgan's yellow teeth were clenched tight against the pain.

'You're getting in someone's way,' he

managed to say.

'I figured that. Hate to think you did this for no good reason.'

'He won't give up.'

'At least we have that in common. Who is he?'

'The hell with you. I ain't saying.'

'Could be a wrong move on your part, if your employer decides leaving you alive is a risk.'

'The hell with you. I'll take my chance in jail.'

There was a scuffle of sound from the mouth of the ally. The shooting had attracted attention and curiosity was rising. Brand stood, still holding the Colt as he turned to face the growing crowd and heard the less than discreet remarks.

'*Ain't that Lex Morgan?*

'*If it is the other must be Brandt. They go around like they was roped together.*'

'*No surprise they got themselves shot.*'

'*Hell it's been waiting to happen.*'

'*Mister, you know you're bleeding?*'

Brand touched fingers to the gash.

A figure pushed his way through the onlookers, a lean, pleasant faced man, eyes taking in the scene. He wore plain clothes and a wide-brimmed low-crown hat. When he saw the gun in Brand's hand he instinctively touched the butt of his own holstered weapon. Light reflected on the star pinned to his shirt. He squared up to Brand.

'You plan on using that again?'

'Wasn't planning to use it at all until this pair forced my hand. Marshal . . . ?'

'Ben Fry's the name and we need to talk about what happened here. Down at my office.'

Brand put away the cut-down Colt and stood waiting while Fry asked for someone to fetch a doctor and the undertaker.

'Tell Doc Holman I'd like him to step down to the office when he's done here. Could a couple of you people escort Morgan to the jail. Doc can see to him in a cell.'

Two men moved forward and hoisted the protesting Morgan to his feet.

'Put him in a cell,' Fry told them. 'Be there shortly.'

He stood looking down at the dead man, shaking his head.

'So who are you?' he said.

'Jason Brand.'

'Follow me, Mister Brand.'

They trailed along the street, Brand drawing curious glances as his bloody face was seen, but Fry kept moving until they reached the stone-built jailhouse. Fry pushed open the thick wooden door, Brand following. By this time Morgan had been secured in one of the jail's empty cells. The men who had brought him left as soon as Fry appeared.

The main office was larger than most, the floor planked. The windows flanking the door had glass in them as well as sturdy iron bars. A desk was angled in the corner facing the door, with a filled gun rack on the solid wall. A couple of high-backed wooden chairs were ranged loosely in front of the desk and Brand smelled the aroma of coffee coming from the enamel pot perched atop the stove in the far corner. A barred door led through to the cells in back where Morgan now resided, making noise until Fry told him to quit, then rejoined Brand. Fry took off his hat and hung it on a wooden peg on the wall over his desk. He gestured at one of the chairs.

'I suggest you sit before you fall down.'

Brand decided that was a helpful suggestion and took one of the chairs. If he had been forced to own up he would have admitted to feeling dizzy.

It was then he noticed another occupant. The man was seated in a chair on the far side of the office. He neither moved or spoke, even when Brand glanced his way. At first Brand figured the man to be Fry's deputy but on closer inspection he realized he knew the face. Unshaven now, but that didn't hide the man's identity. From the photograph

Senator Beauchamp had furnished.

Henry Quinlan.

The Senator's man. Who had initiated the investigation into Elias Bodine's activities.

'Quinlan,' Brand said. 'I've been looking for you a while.'

'You know him?' asked Fry.

'Only by reputation. Senator Beauchamp's missed you and I've been trailing across Texas and running into all kinds of opposition. Friend, you really stirred up a hornet's nest.'

Quinlan stared at the blood running down Brand's face.

'That because of me?'

'Most likely.'

Fry crossed to the stove and poured coffee into china mugs, handing one to Brand and Quinlan. He sat in the swivel seat behind the desk.

'Let me tell you a story,' Fry said. 'About a man who works from the Justice Department based in Washington. Been following a trail after a train robbery back in Handy. He's been following that trail and it's brought him here to Redigo. And as soon as he hits town a couple of local misfits attack him. All that seems to tie in with what Mister Quinlan told me when he showed up in my office. Tell me if I missed something.'

'You're doing fine. I take it you've had contact with my home office?' Brand said.

Fry leaned forward and picked up a couple of buff telegram messages. He slid them across the desk for Brand to read. The messages were from Frank McCord.

'Man doesn't waste words,' Fry said. 'Straight to the point.'

'That's the man.'

'You've met the Senator?' Quinlan said.

'The Senator knows my boss. Went to him with the whole story. My boss called me in and here we are.'

Brand ran through what had taken place since leaving Washington and making his hectic train ride to Handy.

Fry and Quinlan listened without interruption.

'Pretty well ties up with what your Mister McCord told me,' Fry added. 'Doesn't give much away, but expects a deal.'

'He does.'

'Redigo can be a rough town. What with all the passing business. The trail crews and the railhead. I'm sure you know how these Texas cow towns run. Takes a lot of hard work keeping things peaceable.'

'I've been in towns like this before,' Brand said. 'No mean feat keeping the lid on.'

Fry sighed. 'Was pretty quiet until you hit town.'

He said it in a light tone and Brand caught the faint smile on his lips.

'Problems seem to be following me close on this,' he said.

'And those problems brought you here to Redigo? Looking for someone?'

'Man called Elias Bodine.'

'*Bodine?* He wanted for something?'

Quinlan said, 'Bodine is the top dog behind this whole thing. It's because of him I've been chasing my tail all over. The evidence he stole from those Pinkerton men will implicate him and his partners in all kinds of criminal activities. People are already dead because of the attempts to conceal that evidence.'

Fry held up a hand. 'You need to give me a moment to take this in. Friend, you know who Bodine is? The man is wealthy. Powerful. And he has a lot of important people he can also call friends. You sure about what you're saying?'

'I wouldn't be here if I wasn't,' Quinlan said.

The marshal shook his head as if it was almost too hard to take in. He drained his coffee, stood and crossed to refill his mug.

'Bodine has interests in a number of enterprises in town,' he said. 'He has a horse ranch about four miles away. Hell of a place. Runs horse herds. A stud business. Man has a big reputation hereabouts. Contributes money to local causes. Is on real friendly terms with the local judge. Spends money as if it's going out of fashion. Paid for a new bell for the church.' He paused for breath. 'And now you ride into town and tell me he's a damned crook — excuse my French — but that's what it boils down to. Now don't get me wrong, Brand, Quinlan, but you got to admit it's a lot to swallow.'

'I'd be cautious myself considering what's just happened.'

The office door opened and the suited figure of the man Brand was told by Fry to be Redigo's doctor, Amos Holman, stepped inside. He was a pale-haired, plain-looking man in his thirties. He glanced at the blood on Brand's face.

'Been hit in the head, I'm guessing,' he said, dropping his medical bag on Fry's desk. 'You the one who took on Morgan and Brandt?'

'Guilty.'

'Careful what you admit to,' Holman said. 'That's the local marshal over there.'

Fry managed a grin. 'Doc, will you go see to Morgan. Stitch up his leg and if he keeps on grumbling put a few in his mouth.'

Holman paused long enough to press a clean bandage against the gash in Brand's head before he went to treat Morgan.

'Keep that in place. Don't want you bleeding all over the floor.'

'Thanks, doc.'

Holman made his way through to the cells.

Fry refilled the coffee mugs and settled himself on the edge of his desk.

'Just as a matter of interest,' the lawman said, 'do you make these wild train rides often?'

'No. This time was unusual.'

'Damn right there. But when you reached Handy the passenger train had already been attacked and this case of documents taken?'

'That's the way of it.'

'If I wasn't in the know I'd have to figure this was one hell of a fairy story.'

'That's the way I feel. Chasing from hell to breakfast and always out of reach. Mister Quinlan, am I wrong thinking you showing up here in Redigo is putting you right in Bodine's sights?' Fry asked.

'That crossed my mind,' Quinlan admitted. 'Pretty sure he'd love to get his hands on me. I can identify the people who talked. He needs to get to them and make sure they don't stand up to be counted.'

Fry's shoulders slumped.

'This gets more complicated with the telling.'

Brand said, 'I figure it's time to uncomplicate it . . . '

The doctor returned to the office. He cleaned Brand's wound and bandaged it before leaving.

'What do you figure to do next?' Fry asked.

From the cell area someone shouted.

152

A yell of pure alarm. The words were punctuated by the heavy blast of a gun. Two shots that filled the jail with its thunderous noise.

Fry pulled his pistol and headed for the cells.

'Stay with Fry,' Brand said as Quinlan pushed to his feet

Brand hesitated for a couple of seconds. Instead of following the lawman he made for the jail's door, yanking it open and stepping outside . . .

Within the next couple of minutes the unexpected events that occurred would become part of Redigo's history, and they had been set in motion when Henry Quinlan walked into Fry's office some time earlier . . .

THE SHOWDOWN

12

Henry Quinlan . . .

He was fully aware of the danger he had placed himself in. He was intelligent enough to understand not to labor under false illusions. His quarry, Elias Bodine, was no fool. He would have surrounded himself with plenty of protection knowing Quinlan was looking for him. Jay Bledsoe would be around for starters, walking in Bodine's shadow. And there would most likely be added threats to be aware of. The man would go to any lengths to protect himself and the information he had got his hands on.

From his window in the rooming house he had booked into Quinlan had a clear view of Redigo's main street. By edging to the side he was able to see the *King Hotel* where, he knew, Bodine was staying. Since arriving in town Quinlan had seen Bodine entering the large building, Bledsoe at his side. The man hadn't spotted Quinlan and even if he had most likely would not have even recognized him.

Quinlan had forgone his normal attire of suit and neat shirt, exchanging them for the garb of a working range hand. Dusty shirt and pants, high boots and a wide-brimmed hat. He had not shaved for a few days and was sporting a dark stubble. Around his neck he wore a loose neckerchief and on his right hip was a holstered Colt pistol. Quinlan was far from being any kind of expert with the weapon, but he wore it because it was the normal thing to do. He was aware of the weapon's presence and had to keep avoiding the urge to hike the thing up from where it rested against his thigh. As disguises went it was far from comfortable but Quinlan was determined to see the matter through. He was not fully convinced he might fool Bodine even though he knew he had to do something.

After the long weeks of tracking down and speaking to the people involved, getting some of the more reluctant ones to impart the information he needed, Henry Quinlan had his evidence. By the time he put it all together his gathered information weighed up to a damning indictment of Elias Bodine's criminal acts. The evidence pointed the finger at a number of men, all in prestigious positions and all of them party to the fraud and corruption Quinlan was determined to present to Washington.

Quinlan understood the risk he was taking. The man he was going after was wealthy. And had just as wealthy people on his side, all of them who would be determined to remain in those positions of power while they indulged their illegal practices. He was one man. Definitely on his own. In effect surrounded by men who would not hesitate to have him removed if it came to remaining undetected.

Although he had presented his case to the authorities in Washington, there was little that could be done until he actually showed them his documented evidence. Which right now was in Bodine's hands. Quinlan understood that evidence was going to be destroyed once Bodine had tracked down and removed the witnesses. That had been why Bodine had orchestrated the theft of the documents from the train taking it to Washington. Quinlan's plan to send the evidence by train, while he drew Bodine off had failed. Somewhere along the line his deception had been discovered, so instead of drawing his persecutors away, he had been left isolated while Bodine's hired guns had raided the train and taken the evidence.

Quinlan had refused to quit. It was not in his nature to give up. He saw the injustice created by Bodine and his group, and his own innate righteous need to expose them pushed him on. If anything the setback only served to intensify his determination. He had come this far. There was no way he was about to back down now.

Damn Bodine and his hired guns. His rich and powerful conspirators. Henry Quinlan was going to have his day — even at the risk of his life.

The distant sound of a locomotive pulling in at the rail depot broke Quinlan's reverie. He turned and looked beyond the rooftops. Saw the black curl of smoke showing as the train eased to a halt.

He hesitated, his mind in turmoil because he wasn't certain how to proceed. Even though he had tracked Bodine here to Redigo he was not much further forward. Bodine would be closely protected by the bodyguard who went everywhere with him. It was not going to be an easy matter getting close to the man.

About to move from the window Quinlan saw one of Bodine's employees, one of his entourage who hung out at the hotel, fetching and carrying for the man. He watched him walk up through town to the rail depot, which stood just behind the last row of buildings. The man met three passengers from the train, spoke briefly with them, then led them back along the street and into the hotel.

The three were dressed identically in long black dusters, wore Derby hats and gave off the impression they were not people to be messed with.

Bodine was making sure he was safe. Drawing in more hired guns. It made Quinlan increasingly determined to keep going.

He left the rooming house and made his way along the street, his eyes constantly on the move. He spotted the town jail. In his mind he considered speaking to Redigo's lawman, asking for his help. He was one man and the urgency of his situation suggested to him that he needed help. Quinlan usually worked solo. He preferred it that way but he was also smart enough to know when he needed help. He decided he would speak to Ben Fry, the town marshal. He understood he was taking a risk. Right now he had little choice.

They were dressed alike in dark suits and pale-striped shirts and string ties, with ankle-length black dusters. They wore shiny half-boots that were polished to the extreme. And each man wore a neat black Derby hat. Two of them sported neat mustaches. The third was clean shaven. When they stepped down from the train they gathered on the platform, keen eyes taking in every detail of their surroundings.

Each of them carried two cases. One for personal items and clothing. One smaller, hard-shelled, that held a broken-down, shortened double-barreled shotgun. They all wore belt guns in hip holsters — no quick-draw instances with these men. The revolvers were .45 caliber Colt Peacemakers, late model, with ivory grips. They might have looked like a trio of travelling businessmen. That might have been partially true.

They did travel.

And they had business in Redigo.

163

But they were not in town to peddle ladies attire. Or bottles of liquor.

They dealt in a single item — and that was lead.

The clean shaven man — Bart Conlan — was in charge.

Ralph Dorn and Ernst Sunderman were his associates.

Appearance aside they were a killing team. Men who plied their trade with ruthless efficiency. As long as they were paid well they would accept any contract. And once set on their mission they never backed away and up until visiting Redigo they had never failed to fulfill their promise.

They were here to meet with Elias Bodine, because Bodine had hired them to make sure his plans went through. He had himself and a group of anxious partners to protect and Bodine was determined that nothing was about to get in his way. Through sheer force of personality Bodine had become the figurehead. The man with the strength of character and the drive to ensure nothing could destroy the group as a whole. If he failed they were all liable to end up behind bars — maybe hanging at the end of a rope. Bodine didn't fool himself into believing they could avoid punishment if the facts came to light. The reverse side of the card they were playing promised an increase of wealth and power when their various enterprises paid off. So the risks they were possibly facing had to be offset against the rewards.

The three travellers were met by one of Bodine's employees and he led them through town to the *King Hotel* where the arranged meeting was to be held. Bodine was waiting in his suite and wasted no time laying out what he wanted.

'Simple enough,' Conlan said. 'You believe this Quinlan is in the area? And Brand? Mister Bodine, Brand is no novice. I know him. Tough son of a bitch. Don't sell him short.'

'Quinlan isn't going to be frightened off if he decides we have the documents. That case over there has the evidence he wants to use against us. Without it he has no proof. And if Brand becomes a threat he can be part of your business.'

Conlan turned to look at the leather case resting on the oak desk.

'Sounds to me you have what you need there. As long as you do Quinlan isn't much of a threat.'

'You have to understand Henry Quinlan,' Bodine said. 'He's a rarity. An honest man who sees it as his mission to expose us all. He may be one man but he will walk through fire and brimstone to do his *duty*. In that respect he's someone to be feared.'

'You feel the same about Brand?'

'I don't pass him over lightly. He was a US Marshal a few years back. Lost his job through some legal mess up. Did some bounty work, then seemed to fade away for a while. Only he showed up again and rumor said he was working for a man named McCord. Shadowy figure from the Justice Department. My sources tell me Brand is some kind of clandestine operative.'

'Not so clandestine if you found out all this about him.'

Bodine allowed a smile. 'Nothing can stay secret forever if you look and listen hard enough. And if you can pay for information. I have friends in high places.'

'You believe this Brand *hombre* is on your trail?'

'Your insight is correct. Yes, I have the feeling Brand is both searching for Quinlan *and* the documents we retrieved.'

'With McCoy shadowing *him*?'

'McCoy is providing close observation. He intends to stay close, masquerading as the diligent Ranger, and if Brand succeeds we can remove Mister Quinlan once we get our hands on him and extract what he knows.'

'And that's why we're here? To deal with Quinlan and Brand. In case this ex-Ranger needs help?' Conlan glanced across the room to where Jay Bledsoe sat in one corner. Silent. Observing. Not intruding but showing a solid presence. 'How does Bledsoe fit in?'

'He's my personal bodyguard. Nothing else. He wont interfere in your business. His job is to protect me exclusively.'

Conlan nodded in Bledsoe's direction. A courtesy from one professional to another. He received a slight return of acknowledgement.

'That's fine, Mister Bodine.'

'Right now I want to leave town,' Bodine said. 'Get out to the ranch. We will be more secure there. I suggest you go to the livery and rent yourselves horses. Just tell the man to charge the costs to my account. Then get back here and we can leave as soon as possible.

Before the three exited the room they slipped out of the dusters and donned leather slings to which they clipped the shotguns after they had assembled and loaded the weapons. The shotguns hung loosely from the slings, then covered by the dusters. Extra shells were dropped into the deep pockets of the dusters.

The arming was carried out quickly and silently, then the trio left without another word.

'Hell of a performance,' Bledsoe said, obviously not impressed. 'Surprised they didn't do it to music.'

Bodine glanced at his bodyguard. 'Quite the cynic, Jay.'

'Never did go in for all that show. You want a man dead you do it fast, not make grand gestures.'

'I'm sure Henry Quinlan would feel better knowing that.'

A short time later Bledsoe crossed to the window and peered out. He stared down at the street, then turned. Saw the three black-clad riders waiting outside the hotel next to Bodine's buggy.

'We can leave any time,' Bledsoe said.

They made their way out of the hotel. Climbed into the buggy.

'Let's go,' Bodine said.

As they passed along the street there was the sound of gunshots coming from an alley. People rushed to see what was happening. Bledsoe slowed the buggy and they saw the town marshal push through the crowd and go into the ally. He emerged alongside a tall, dark-haired man with a blood-streaked face.

'That's Brand,' Conlan said. 'I know his face.'

They kept moving. Out beyond town and picking up the trail that would lead them to Bodine's horse ranch.

Although they left Redigo behind, they didn't leave their problems, as they were to find out before they had travelled far.

★　★　★

It had gone easier than he had anticipated. After he had shot Morgan through the barred cell window, McCoy had slipped from the alley beside the jail and made a quick move across the rear of the building next to it before emerging back on the street. He moved cautiously, not wanting to attract any undue attention as people began to converge outside the jail. The crowd were too curious to find out what had happened to even notice as McCoy slipped from the distant alley. And walked calmly across the street.

He was satisfied he had made certain the man named Morgan would not offer up his name if questioned. It would have been better if Brand had killed both his attackers following their abortive attack. They hadn't so McCoy had been forced to make a risky move in order to silence Morgan. A couple of shots through the cell's barred window and Morgan was no more.

A reckless, unplanned move perhaps, not something McCoy would normally have done. But he'd had little choice. His commitment was absolute. He accepted his time working for Bodine was over. The man had already paid McCoy so he wasn't leaving with empty pockets. Now he needed to leave. To make good his escape and head west, far away from Texas.

Almost halfway across the street. McCoy allowed himself to relax.

That was until a familiar voice reached him.

'Been wondering where you got to,' Brand said.

McCoy slowed. Turned to face Brand.

'Had official business to attend to. Ranger business.'

'McCoy, we both know that isn't so. There is no Ranger business any more.'

McCoy saw Brand facing him. Hatless. The side of his face streaked with blood. A thin bandage around his head.

'What is it you're saying, boy?'

'You want me to spell it out? This whole damn act has nothing to do with the Rangers, McCoy. You were kicked out. Let go because you broke the law and the Rangers dismissed you.'

McCoy knew there was no walking away now. Much as he hated to admit it Brand had him dead to rights. He reached up with his hand and yanked the Ranger badge from his shirt, casting it aside.

'Damnation, son, you got it right

enough. This isn't about the Rangers. *This is about me, W.J. McCoy, goddam you.'*

Brand could have mentioned the fact McCoy had turned his back on his Ranger service. All the years he had spent tracking and dealing with outlaws. Bringing in wanted men because that was his job. He didn't. He saw no reason to waste his time and energy on a man who had already crossed the line and accepted there was no turning back. McCoy had chosen his path. He was committed to it and Brand was standing in his way.

'Brand, I'd expect you to understand. Look what they did to you. Took your badge and pushed you out. That piece of tin don't mean shit in the end.'

'Doesn't compare. And I damnwell don't need to justify myself to you, McCoy. This isn't about me. It's about you and just killing a man in his jail cell.'

'A loose end is all.'

Brand saw the way the man tensed,

hands moving with fractional slowness so they were over the butts of the big Walker Colt pistols. McCoy showed nothing in his face. His eyes were fixed. Expressionless as he stared directly at Brand.

'No need for us to take this any further. All I want is Quinlan. I have to find him. Give him up to Bodine. That's my ticket out of this life.'

'One man's life for your own?'

'I guess that's what it comes down to.'

'Proves one thing,' Brand said.

'What?'

'Just how low you've sunk, McCoy.'

'You *judge* me?' For the first time a flicker of emotion showed in McCoy's eyes. 'Forgotten how I saved your life back in Blanco?'

'Only reason you did was because it suited your plan. Wasn't because you felt any obligation.'

'They say every good deed has a way of turning back on you . . . '

On the edge of Brand's vision he saw

McCoy's thumbs lift slightly and he knew the man was about to draw. As his hands went back his thumbs would reach his gun hammers first, drawing them back to cock the Dragoons even as he cleared leather. It was a smart move, intended to give the shooter an advantage over a slower draw, only Brand had seen the action and he knew well enough to stay ahead.

His right hand fell, his own move seeming unhurried, but there was a deadly intent in his response. In his mind was a recollection of something the department armorer, Whitehead, had told him when Brand had first met him. About accuracy in placing his shot being more important than displaying too much speed. Brand had held that belief and it had proved its worth on more than one occasion.

McCoy had to lift the not inconsiderable weight of the big pistols. Bringing them up on line despite clearing his holsters quickly. The nearly five-pound drag of those massive weapons had to have a slowing effect, marginal as it was, and it became the difference.

Brand brought his Peacemaker on line. Held for a beat. Arm extended and his finger curled against the slight trigger pull. The Colt hammered out its sound. Spat a sliver of flame. The .45 caliber lead slug hit McCoy chest high and cored in deep. Brand put a second shot into the man and this was into the heart.

McCoy took a faltering step back, his face registering shock, his body arching in response to what had happened. The left-hand pistol thundered as his finger reflectively jerked the trigger. The big slug tore against his leg as he began to fall, slamming to the ground heavily.

'Jesus,' Quinlan said, 'he meant to kill you.'

He was outside the jail, staring at McCoy's body. Brand turned, catching hold of the man's sleeve.

'We don't get off this street that could still happen.'

'But . . .'

'Move, *damnit*,' Brand growled. 'Ain't as if I don't like you, but I figure catching a bullet on your behalf is way beyond doing my duty.'

He pushed Quinlan forward, back inside the jail. Just as they reached the door Fry showed himself, cradling a Greener shotgun in his arms. The moment they were through the door Fry slammed it shut, turning to eye his visitors.

'Damndest thing I seen in a long time,' he said. 'The telling about W.J. McCoy had him as fast with those Walkers.'

Brand was shucking the used cartridges from the Colt and replacing them.

'Isn't the speed,' he said, 'it's where you put your bullets.'

'Well I seen it,' Fry went on, 'and damned if *I* barely believe it.'

'What about Morgan?' Brand asked.

Fry shook his head. 'He's dead.'

Brand glanced across at Quinlan. 'You still want those documents?'

'It's what I came for.'

Fry, realizing Brand's intentions,

said, 'He left town. Bodine. He was in that fancy black buggy he owns. All lettered with the name of the stud. Not something a body could miss. Just before you braced McCoy. Had Jay Bledsoe at his side, and three black-clad fellers who come in on the morning train were riding alongside.'

'Which way did they go?'

'I'd say they were heading for Bodine's horse ranch few miles out of town.'

'He got more guns out there?'

'Only the hands he pays to tend his stock. They're no gun fighters.'

'That still leaves four who are,' Quinlan said.

'Nobody ever said this job was going to be easy,' Brand said. 'I was told to get that evidence back. If Bodine has it it'll be close.'

He took up the rifle he had left in Fry's office and checked it was fully loaded.

'You can't just ride out there and ask for it back,' Fry said.

'Who said anything about *asking*?'

13

Now . . .

'You hear that?'

Bledsoe eased back on the reins, turning his head.

'Hear what?' Bodine asked.

'Gunfire is what,' Bart Conlan said. He had reined in his horse alongside the buggy. 'From town.'

Bodie managed a slight smirk. 'This is Texas. Redigo is a cow town. What do you expect?'

'Couple of shots from a Walker. Dragoon. Little while later two shots from a .45. And one more from a Walker.'

'You can tell that from this distance?'

'Guns are my business, Mister Bodine. Day I can't tell the difference is when I put mine away.'

'McCoy carries .44 Walkers,' Bledsoe said.

'So McCoy bracing Brand?' Bodine said. 'I recall we've been expecting that.'

Conlan glanced at his partners.

'Ernst go and find out what happened.'

Bodine said, 'If the chance shows itself deal with Brand. I'm tired of hearing his damn name.'

Conlan gave a slight nod and Sunderman reined about and picked up the way back to Redigo.

'Might just be our chance,' he said.

They continued on their journey and reached the ranch a while later.

It was a well maintained, impressive sight. Corrals and a big Dutch barn. Outbuildings, with a long bunkhouse for the crew. A cook house stood nearby. Horses were roaming the corrals and Bodine's crew went about their business. The whole place displayed a sense of purpose.

Standing across the hard-packed yard was the large ranch house itself. An imposing three-story structure that combined stone and timber. A railed gallery ran around the second floor. The timber sections were painted in a deep maroon with white trim. The house exuded wealth. A status symbol for Bodine's position.

'Pretty nice place,' Conlan said.

Bodine led the way inside, with Bledsoe close, Conlan and Dorn following behind. A Mexican dressed in pristine whites appeared, taking Bodine's hat.

'In the study, Mateo. Coffee.'

The Mexican nodded and padded away as Bodine led his guests through a wide door into the room beyond. A large window looked out over the ranch yard. Bodine crossed and took his place behind his large desk, a wave of his hand indicating everyone could sit. As usual Bledsoe sat in a chair close to his employer. Saying nothing. Simply observing.

'What do you believe your man will find in town?' Bodine asked.

Conlan shrugged.

It was Bledsoe who unexpectedly broke the silence.

'I'd say a surprise,' he said with conviction.

Sunderman rode in to find Redigo going about its business with little regard to what had taken place only a short time ago. He took his horse to the hitch rail outside one of the larger saloons and dismounted. He stepped up on the walk and took a slow look around. He gave himself time to cover the whole of the street until he was convinced he wasn't about to find any answers there. Turning he pushed through the batwings and went inside.

The interior was cooler than on the street. Sunderman took off his Derby and ran a hand through his hair. Sleeved the beads of sweat from his brow. His appearance drew marginal interest. The half full saloon was too busy with its own concerns.

Sunderman moved to the long, polished bar and caught the eye of one of the bartenders.

'What would you like?'

'Beer.'

182

Sunderman observed the crowd behind him through the wide mirror on the wall behind the bar. He waited until the beer was placed in front of him. Dropped money on the bar. He picked it up and took a taste. It eased the dryness in his throat.

'New in town?'

Sunderman looked up from his glass.

'Came in on the morning train. On my way to Bodine's place. Looking for work. He's been asking around for a bookkeeper.'

'Could do worse. Bodine's a big man around here.'

'Don't say.'

'If you come in on the train you must have heard the shootin' earlier.'

Sunderman nodded. 'Heard from my hotel room. What happened?'

'Man in the jail was shot. Then a couple fellers got into some kind of ruckus. Had them a drawdown.'

'Anyone hurt bad?'

'Bad as it can get. One feller got himself killed.'

'That bad, huh. Local?'

'No. Way I heard the deceased was a feller name of McCoy.'

'What about t'other man?'

'He come out without a scratch from what I heard.'

Sunderman listened, taking it all in as he supped his beer. The bartender, like many of his kind, was the fount of all local knowledge. As well as serving drinks he absorbed and passed out information. Almost as good as a local newspaper — but without bias.

'And I missed it,' Sunderman said. 'This feller who *didn't* get shot — he a local?'

'Newcomer too. From what I heard he got into a scrape earlier and put a couple of local misfits down who tried to rob him. Busted a cap and blew a feller's head apart. That's the story I heard. Somebody saw this shooter and another feller visiting the jail with the town lawman, Ben Fry. Odd thing was, from what I heard, they were being real sociable with each other. Other man

184

was a stranger in town as well.'

'And there I was thinking Redigo was a quiet town.'

The bartender chuckled, said, 'Never be all that peaceable being a cow town and all. But she's been busier than normal last day or so.'

Sunderman finished his beer. He squared his hat and took a final glance around the saloon.

'Obliged,' he said and made his way outside.

He paused, gazing along the street in the direction of the jail.

He was convinced now that the man involved in the shootings had to be Jason Brand. Seemed a logical conclusion with the man seemingly talking freely to the local law.

In the company of a second newcomer to Redigo.

The name came into Sunderman's mind without any kind of encouragement.

Henry Quinlan.

Sunderman shook his head. Could they be that lucky? Having Quinlan show up on Brand's heels.

Well, he thought, *they would no doubt find the answer to that soon enough.*

He moved along the boardwalk, one hand slipping beneath his duster to grasp the sling-hanging shotgun. His fingers stroked the smooth metal, eased down to the silky wood of the stock. A thin smile edged his lips as he felt the cool silkiness of the wood.

Brand.

Quinlan.

The town lawman.

A nice neat threesome. He gripped the shotgun, the closest thing to pleasure coursing through his body. Sunderman had a thing about anyone who represented the law. Put simply he didn't like them. Most of his adult life he had clashed with the law in one form or another. They had put him in jail twice. Bad places where worse things happened. Sunderman never forgot those things. His fingers closed against the shotgun. Time for a reckoning. Time for him to make his play.

14

'I've had a prisoner die in the cells from natural causes,' Fry said. 'Never had one shot through the damn window.'

Morgan had been taken away by the undertaker a little while ago but Fry was still unnerved by what had happened. McCoy's body had also been moved from the street.

Fry was standing at one of the office windows. Looking along the street.

'You want to take a look here,' he said.

Brand joined him 'What am I looking at?'

'Feller standing outside the *Lucky Lady*. Long black duster. Derby hat.'

'I see him.'

'Tell me I'm wrong but he looks like one of the three who came in on the morning train. They were met by one of Bodine's men and he led them to the hotel where Bodine has a permanent suite. Last seen they were riding alongside Bodine's buggy when he left town. All three of them wore those dusters and Derby hats. No law against that but just something about them don't sit right.'

Brand watched the man move along the boardwalk. Even at a distance the deliberate way the man was treading the boardwalk, his gaze fixed directly on the jail, advertised his intention.

'*Son of a bitch,*' Brand said softly.

The man suddenly pulled his black duster open and exposed the sling-hung twin barreled shotgun. He pulled it around and held it in plain sight.

'I know you're in there, Brand. Show yourself, mister,' he said.

Quinlan said, 'He's coming on. What are you going to do?'

'Oblige the man,' he said. 'Not much room in here to hide. And I don't like what scatter guns can do.'

He lifted the latch and pulled the jail door wide. He laid the rifle down, not wanting to be encumbered by it. He pulled the Colt and held it tight against his stomach.

'*Don't be . . .* ' Fry said.

His words were lost as Brand moved forward, through the door and across the boardwalk, increasing his pace as he reached the edge. A fleeting thought ran through his mind as he left the walk, of Kito and his punishing training sessions. His determination to drill into Brand the means of surviving confrontations. The way to move. To fall without injuring himself. Those moves were not something Brand used a great deal, but the repetitive practice came to mind as he launched himself clear of the boardwalk, the dusty surface of the street coming up to meet him. He threw out his left hand and let it guide him into a shoulder roll.

As you fall, make shoulder roll, let it absorb the impact so you do not harm yourself.

The man's soft voice seemed to follow as Brand felt the ground slide beneath him, executing a smooth follow through, coming up on one knee, his gunhand clearing his chest.

Dust billowed up around Brand.

As he turned his body, the Colt following he caught a glimpse of the black-clad man, swinging his own form around on the boardwalk. The long duster flew back like a rippling cloak, as Sunderman pulled the shotgun around and fired.

Brand felt the impact as the burst hit the ground feet away, raising chunks of dirt. He felt the hot sting as stray shot caught the outer flesh of his left thigh. Then he heard the hard boom of the shot, the deep, throaty sound loud in his ears.

By this time he had the pistol on target, hammer already back. He tracked in on Sunderman's lean body, eased back on the trigger and felt the Colt buck as it fired.

The .45 slug hit Sunderman in the chest and he took a faltering step back, face registering surprise. Even so he jerked the shotgun back at Brand. Too slow as Brand cocked and fired again and a third time. Sunderman was turned sideways on, stumbling across the boardwalk and thumped against the wall. His legs gave and he slithered down, the redundant shotgun discharging its second load into the walk. Sunderman hunched over, his head wedged against the wall. Blood was dripping from his chest.

As Fry stepped out from the jail, gun in his hand, Quinlan close behind, Brand pushed to his feet, his Colt still held on Sunderman. He sensed movement along the street as onlookers began to gather. Brand ignored them. As long as none of them were dressed in black dusters and wearing Derby hats he didn't give a damn.

'That was some fancy move,' Fry said.

Brand concentrated on reloading his Colt, carefully thumbing in fresh cartridges, pretending he didn't notice the slight tremble in his hands.

Son of a bitch, it never got any easier.

Fry stood over the body. He moved the shotgun aside with his foot.

'I'll be damned,' he said, 'you see that? His Derby never came off.'

'You're bleeding,' Quinlan said.

Brand glanced down and saw the patch of blood on his pants where the stray shot had hit. Now he could feel the fiery sting from the wound.

'That's getting to be normal for this job.'

'Let's get you to my office,' Fry said.

He sent someone to tell the undertaker what had happened. Quinlan followed close behind as they moved along the street.

'I reckon I've brought nothing but problems with me,' he said.

Brand looked over his shoulder. 'You expecting Bodine and his bunch to go down easy?'

'I didn't want all this.'

'None of us want it,' Brand said, 'but it's what we've got.'

The doctor showed up minutes later. He dropped his bag on Fry's desk and stood over Brand.

'Good thing I don't have any other patients,' he said dryly. 'Leg this time.'

'You don't miss a thing, doc,' Fry said.

'I hope this isn't going to be a regular occurrence, Mister Brand, because you'll be running out of body parts. Now would you kindly let down your pants.'

Holman took three lead shot out of Brand's thigh. They hadn't penetrated too deep but it was an uncomfortable experience as the doctor used steel tweezers to work the pellets out. He cleaned the holes with antiseptic that stung as much as the wounds. After he had bound the leg and washed his hands he took a mug of coffee from Fry.

'It appears to me we have an ongoing problem here in Redigo. From what you've been telling me Elias Bodine has a lot to answer for.'

Brand had pulled on his remaining pair of pants from his saddlebags. He glanced up from buckling on his gun-belt.

'Bodine paying for his misdemeanors is top of my list, Doc.'

'Should I stock up on my medical supplies?'

'The way things are you might well just do that.'

'And telling you to go easy on that leg for a while?'

Brand picked up his rifle. 'Thanks for the concern, doc. Much appreciated.'

Holman sighed, understanding. He took his bag and left the office.

'We leaving now?' Quinlan said.

'We?'

'Mister Brand, Bodine is anxious to meet me. I wouldn't want to disappoint him.'

Fry had picked himself a rifle from the wall rack. He passed it to Quinlan, then took a second for himself.

'Somebody has to watch your back, Mister Brand. I wouldn't feel right not doing that.'

15

Ralph Dorn was pacing across the ranch yard when Conlan came out of the house. He was carrying his shotgun in the crook of his arm and he faced Conlan with a nervous expression on his face.

'Why's it taking Ernst so long to get back from town? Been hours now. All he had to do was take a look around.'

'Taking his sweet time is all,' Conlan said. His tone said different.

'No,' Dorn said. 'He wouldn't do that. Hell, Bart, you know Ernst. He doesn't waste time. I say he should have been back before this.'

'Nothing we can do about that now. We're being paid to look out for Bodine. He's here. So are we.'

'And where is everyone? This spread is like a ghost town. All I seen is that feller in the cook shack. Thought this was a working ranch.'

'That's where the crew is. Out working the range. Bodine's orders. It's what they do. Ease off, Ralph.' Conlan grinned. 'Take a lesson from those horses in the corral over there. Stay nice and loose.'

Conlan went back inside the house.

Dorn shook his head, turned and moved across the yard, his eyes sweeping back and forth as he checked the area. He didn't care what Conlan said. He felt uneasy. Apart from the sound of the horses milling around in the corral and the gentle rustle of the leaves on the cottonwoods that edged the far side of the yard the place was too quiet. Dorn liked at least some kind of noise from activity. This place had the subdued atmosphere of a graveyard.

He reached the barn. Paused and turned on his heels as he saw movement out by the trees. *Or thought he saw movement*. Damned trees with their swaying branches and leaves. They cast shadows that interwove and played tricks. Trouble was the longer he stared Dorn couldn't make out real from false. In the end he turned away. Now he needed a drink. It was hot out in the open, with the heat of the sun bearing down on him. A thought crossed his mind. Maybe that was why Sunderman hadn't got back yet. He was in a saloon back in Redigo having himself a beer. Or two beers. Taking his time before he made the dusty ride out to Bodine's place. He might even be spending some time with one of the girls in the saloon. Sunderman liked the ladies. Figured himself some kind of Romeo. A grin formed on Dorn's lips.

Yeah, that could be it. Sunderman was dallying with some girl. Buying her favors and hoping to . . .

That couldn't be right. It was definitely not right. Or fair. Not with Dorn having to spend his time walking around in the heat, almost parched 'cause he needed a drink himself. He cast around and spotted the pump that was positioned near the cook shack. He made his way over. The cast iron pump fed a small stone basin. Dorn let his shotgun dangle by its sling as he took off his hat and placed it on the lip of the basin, then began to work the pump handle. The pump was well maintained and worked smoothly. After a few pumps cool water began to issue from the wide mouth of the pump. Dorn leaned over and took a mouthful. At least the water was cool and tasted fresh out of the ground. He slaked his thirst, then ducked his head under the stream and let the water splash over his hair and face. Satisfied he stood upright, shaking his head to get rid of the excess water like a dog just out of a rainstorm. He used both hands to slick back his hair and reached for his hat.

That was when he saw the horse and rider coming into sight from beyond the trees. It was moving at a walk.

Dorn crossed the yard.

He had recognized the horse as the tall gray Sunderman had been riding.

And he recognized the rider . . . it

was his partner . . . but there was something wrong.

Sunderman was sitting upright, head down on his chest, his only movement a gentle sway from side to side.

Dorn gripped the shotgun as he crossed the yard.

'*Jesus* . . .'

It was Ernst Sunderman. No doubt there. But he was dead as any man could be with three bloody bullet holes in his chest, wrists tied to the saddle horn and his boots to the stirrups. When he got close enough to the horse Dorn was able to look up at Sunderman's face. His eyes were still open, showing a glassy stare and his face had a deathly, near gray cast to it. Sunderman's slack jaw had let his tongue bulge between his teeth.

'*Bart*,' Dorn yelled out. 'Get yourself back out here. And be quick about it.'

When Conlan saw Sunderman he stood silently, fists at his sides clenching and unclenching. He didn't say anything for a while. He had taken off his duster and Derby hat while in the house but still carried his slung shotgun and had his holstered Colt around his waist.

'All he had to do was look and listen,' he said eventually. 'What the hell did he do to make this happen?'

'Whoever did for him wanted us to know,' Dorn said. 'Could be they're out there watching right now. Ernst didn't make it all the way from town like this. Somebody roped him to his saddle and pointed him here.'

'How many do you figure?'

'This man Brand for certain. Maybe Quinlan. He'll want his documents back.'

'Just two? Not a posse?'

'Uh-huh. They'll do this on their own. Not bring in a noisy bunch of riders.'

Conlan turned and made his way to the porch. The house main door stood ajar, with the dark shape of Jay Bledsoe standing back.

'Not going quite as well as you

expected,' he said, glancing beyond Conlan to where the motionless horse and its dead rider stood. 'Bodine isn't going to be happy.'

'Well that shakes me up all to hell. You just go and tell him we have things under control.'

Bledsoe failed to hold back a cold smile. 'Yeah. I can see that.'

He turned away and moved back inside the house, pushing the door shut as he dismissed Conlan.

Conlan flicked his shotgun into place, easing back the hammers until they locked in position.

'Ralph, go check around the back of the house. Make sure they haven't snuck in that way.'

Dorn nodded. 'No cover back there,' he said. 'All flat ground.'

'Check it anyway.'

Dorn vanished around the side of the house, leaving Conlan on his own. He stared at the dead man on the horse. Had to give it to the man Brand. A nice move to send in Sunderman's corpse as a quiet reminder he was around. If Conlan had been the superstitious kind it could have unnerved him. But he wasn't and it didn't. He turned his attention to the line of cottonwoods, branches moving in the warm breeze that had sprung up. The breeze also stirred up the yard's dry dust, sending a thin swirl of it into view. Like Dorn had been caught up in the ripple of shadows in amongst the trees Conlan stepped forward a few paces, wanting to make sure they were only shadows.

He had almost convinced himself there was nothing when he picked out a flash of color in amongst the shadows.

Something red. Like a man's shirt.

'*Goddamn it*,' he mouthed. 'Dorn — get the hell back here.'

He swung the shotgun on line, tripping one trigger, then turned about and stepped behind the bulk of Sunderman's horse. He moved the length of the horse, aimed and loosed off the second barrel. He broke the action and plucked out the smoking shells, fishing fresh loads from his shirt pocket and dropped them in place. Reloaded he crouched, peering around the nervous horse's flanks.

Where the hell was Dorn?

The man appeared, clearing the corner of the ranch house.

'The trees,' Conlan yelled. '*They're in the goddam trees.*'

And that was when it all happened . . .

* * *

Fry was able to direct them to the ranch by way of a route that kept them out of sight and a quarter mile rom the outfit they tethered their horses and completed the approach on foot. Brand led the horse that carried Sunderman's body, now roped into place to keep him in the saddle. He wanted to use the horse and rider as a distraction while he, Fry and Quinlan moved in unobserved. They quartered in the deep stand of cottonwoods that fringed the ranch yard and checked the area.

There was a single man on watch. Black clad in a long duster, Derby hat on his head and a cut-down shotgun in his hands.

'Looks to be one of those who arrived on the train,' Fry said. 'If they're here I'm certain sure Bodine is in the house.'

Brand finished securing the ropes holding Sunderman on the horse's back.

'We need to spread apart. If things get heated we'll have guns firing our way.'

'Good thought,' Quinlan said.

'Fry,' Brand said. 'Before we move take off that badge you're wearing. Sunlight hits that metal it'll be like a damn signal. It'll make you an easy target.'

Fry glanced down at the burnished badge pinned to his shirt. 'Never thought of that.'

He unpinned the badge and put it into one of his pockets.

'Let's do this,' Brand said.

He led the horse and its silent rider to the edge of the cottonwood stand to where the beaten trail led down into the ranch yard. He draped the reins over the animal's neck, then gave it a solid whack on the rump and set it forward. The horse cantered in the direction of the yard, its interest caught by the corralled horses moving about restlessly.

From where he stood in the shadows of the timber Brand saw the armed man spot the horse. Heard him call out to the house. He watched as a second man came outside. Both men stared at the horse and its dead rider.

The distraction allowed Brand and his partners to move, spacing themselves out. The distraction didn't last for long. One of the men moved around the ranch house to check the rear of the property.

The remaining man, coat- and hatless, moved forward, scanning the trees, and his relaxed stance altered as he spotted something.

He yelled out to his partner, then

triggered his shotgun, the blast peppering the trunks of the cottonwoods.

Quinlan gave a startled cry as lead shot clipped his left arm. Fragments of cloth blew from his sleeve, followed by bloody flesh. He dropped to his knees, clamping a hand to his arm a fraction of a second before a second blast came from the shooter.

'Stay down,' Brand yelled.

Out the corner of his eye he saw the second shotgunner move back into view from the side of the house. As he broke cover Brand saw the man's weapon lift as he kept coming. Brand brought the Winchester to his shoulder, sighting quickly. He triggered a shot and saw a spurt of dust rise from the shotgunner's torso. The man paused but kept coming, his shotgun raised. They fired together. Brand felt the hot sting of the shot across his left side. The jolt only served to force Brand's hand. He had already levered another round into the rifle's breech and he triggered the shot, placing the .44–40 slug into the gunner's midsection, then followed with a close spaced double burst from the Winchester that put the shooter down hard.

As Brand moved to engage, Fry stepped by him, his gaze centered on the man who had fired at Quinlan. With his shotgun empty the man realized he had no time to reload, so he cast the weapon aside and drew his holstered Colt with a smooth action, turning the weapon at Fry as Redigo's lawman came on.

Both men fired. The crash of shots was followed by more. The hard sounds echoed even as follow-up shots came.

Fry twisted under the impact of a .45 slug that cracked a couple of ribs. He pressed a hand over the wound and raised his pistol again.

Conlan, the lawman's target, saw Dorn go down from Brand's Winchester, then felt a slug thump into his left side chest from Fry's gun. He pulled himself upright, drawing his muzzle on Fry for another shot. It never came. Brand had angled his Winchester around and he pumped a fast trio of .44–40 slugs into the man. Conlan slipped to his knees so that Fry's already committed shot ripped into and through his neck. Blood began to bubble from a severed artery as Conlan dropped.

'*The house*,' Quinlan said. '*Bodine*.'

He broke into a run, passing Brand and Fry, his pistol in his hand, ignoring Brand's warning to hold back. He made directly for the front door, his determination to confront Bodine swamping any thoughts of safety.

'*Quinlan, back away*,' Brand yelled. He let his rifle slip to the ground and drew his Colt.

Quinlan was deaf to any warnings. He reached the verandah steps. As he did the house door swung open and Jay Bledsoe filled the frame, his Colt in his hand. The bodyguard fired without hesitation, dropping the hammer on two bullets. The close-range shots slammed into Quinlan and kicked him back off the steps, his own weapon flying unused from his hand.

Brand and Fry leveled their weapons and fired almost as one. Bledsoe jerked under the multiple impact of the slugs, his body slamming against the door-frame. He tried to bring his weapon back on line again. Brand aimed and fired again, putting his shot into Bledsoe's chest and the man pitched face down on the porch in a slack heap.

'Help him,' Brand said to Fry.

He went up to the door and stepped inside. He paused in the hall. Picked up noise to his left and moved to the closed door. He booted it open, sending the door swinging wide. It crashed back, one hinge tearing free.

The room beyond was dominated by a large oak desk and chairs. Walls adorned with bookshelves and hunting trophies. Rifles and shotguns in a glass fronted cabinet. It was a room that displayed the dominance of the man who resided there.

Elias Bodine had abandoned any pretense of his power as he made an abortive attempt at burning the sheaf of documents piled on the floor at his feet. He held an oil lamp in one hand, struggling to loosen the filler cap. His face glistened with sweat as he fumbled with the metal cap. He turned to stare at Brand.

'I can't let you take them,' he said. 'Too many people could be hurt . . . '

'Too many already have been hurt,' Brand said.

The dead at the scene of the robbery. Killed because they were simply in the way.

Henry Quinlan and Ben Fry.

Too many damaged to conceal the crimes of Elias Bodine and his partners.

There was no way the man was going to escape from that.

The Colt's hammer snapped back.

The shot was loud thunder in the room.

Brand slumped in one of the chairs, blood soaking through his shirt, the pistol suddenly heavy in his hand.

He barely noticed when Fry appeared in the doorway. The lawman's shirt was

210

sodden with his own blood. He leaned against the door frame. He saw the document's on the floor. Bodine's body stretched out across the boards, the back of his skull open and ragged where Brand's slug had shattered it.

'Quinlan didn't make it,' he said quietly. 'Hell of a price to pay for a pile of papers. Washington had better make good use of them.'

'They will,' Brand said. 'I'll make sure they do . . . '

16

In the couple of weeks that followed there was a flurry of activity. Despite the Justice Department attempting to contain the details in the evidence Henry Quinlan had compiled, news got out and people named by the witnesses made attempts to distance themselves from the consequences. Arrests followed. Two of the accused committed suicide. Others tried to flee from custody. The information Quinlan had gathered was detailed. Meticulous. And his powers of persuasion brought witnesses forward ready to talk and point the finger. There were attempts to silence those talking, but in the end, the truth came out and the courts wielded their power and handed down heavy verdicts.

Henry Quinlan's family was informed of his death and the important part he had played in the downfall of the people involved. No amount of praise was going to bring Quinlan back, but his relatives were made aware of his courageous sacrifice.

Ben Fry recovered from his wounds and resumed his duties as marshal of Redigo.

Likewise Jason Brand returned to Washington and made his report to Frank McCord, who rewarded him with a couple of weeks rest before returning him to duty. Brand figured he had come out of it all with an easy result.

There had been some minor upset with the Texas Rangers when McCord informed them McCoy had been *dealt with*, as he put it. The fuss was more to do with the fact Brand had done their job for them. The Rangers had a proud tradition of dealing with Ranger problems by themselves. McCoy turning his back on the force had not gone down too well, but they had to admit he had done them a service by ridding them of a man who had broken the Ranger code.

Brand had received a letter from Adam, informing him that his son and Virginia Maitland would be returning to America in a few weeks. That was the best news he could have had.

Before his return to Washington Brand had made a visit to Handy where he spoke to Hicks and Toby Books. It was a closure of sorts for them to know that the men who had staged the train robbery had been dealt with. After his visit Brand met up with Jake Converse. The stable owner was happy to see Brand. And pleased to see Lady was unharmed. Something in Brand's manner suggested there was more to his visit. An hour later, money having changed hands, Brand left the stable as the new owner of the paint. Converse had made a big thing of how he favored the horse and wouldn't want to lose her, but he was in the end a businessmen and following a protracted haggling session both men got what they wanted. Converse hurried off to the bank with his money and Brand went to the depot to arrange for his and Lady's passage on the first train out of Handy.

Brand had a long ride ahead of him. Enough time to consider that now he had two females on his hands. One might have had four legs and an attitude, but he figured between them they were going to keep him well occupied with their individual demands.

Settling in his seat as the train pulled out of Handy, with Lady secure in the livery coach, it came to him that the near future was going to be a busy time — and added to that he still had Frank McCord to keep him on his toes . . .

BALLARD & MCCALL:
TWO FROM TEXAS
GUNS OF THE BRASADA
COLORADO BLOOD HUNT
COLTER'S QUEST